About the Author

When Barbara Wilson graduated from Edinburgh University in 1988, she decided she was going to explore the world. She began teaching English in the south of Italy and fell quickly under its spell as well as falling in love with the handsome Italian man she eventually married. She lives in the heel of Italy to this day.

D1333501

Dedication

To Christina Wilson, my beloved mother, whose constant inspiration and love continues to illuminate and enrich my life.
To Marcello Gargiulo, my dear husband, whose Italian exuberance captured my heart.

Barbara Wilson

HOUSE OF SECRETS

AUSTIN MACAULEY
PUBLISHERS LTD.

A CIP catalogue record for this title is available from the British Library.

ISBN 9781785543487 (Paperback)
ISBN 9781785543494 (Hardback)
ISBN 9781785543500 (E-Book)

www.austinmacauley.com

First Published (2016)
Austin Macauley Publishers Ltd.
25 Canada Square
Canary Wharf
London
E14 5LQ

Acknowledgments

With special thanks to all of my family, who have always loved me and given their support.

With grateful thanks to my publishers for giving me this opportunity to see my very first novel in print.

PART 1

CHAPTER 1

ROMAN HOLIDAY

More than fifteen years had passed since Emily Crespi had last set foot in Rome. There had been a small group of language teachers at the school near the Pantheon where she used to work, all young women, some of whom had arrived in Italy with the express intention of marrying Italians and settling permanently in the Eternal City. Of course Emily had an Italian boyfriend too but she had considered herself too wise and worldly at the time not to call off their engagement at the very last moment and make her escape all the way back to grey Britain. She could still remember the sight of tears welling up in Piero Nisi's big brown eyes when she had told him she was leaving him; they had been in one of their favourite restaurants on the banks of the Tiber, not very far from the much more opulent restaurant she found herself in now.

The company was somewhat different tonight of course. Dottor Cellamare was all sleek black hair (that Emily suspected was dyed), manicured nails and expensive scent. He smoked a lot, making a great show of his gold Dupont lighter every time he lit up a cigarette, entirely oblivious to the "No Smoking" sign at his back. He made it perfectly obvious he found Emily's presence intrusive, interested as he was only in

Grazia, whom he prodded and teased for the duration of the meal. Emily was thoroughly depressed by the lack of manners of her table companions and wished herself elsewhere. Toni Cellamare made ribald remarks that had Grazia giggling appreciatively like a silly schoolgirl. It was not at all an auspicious start to Emily's holiday. She had somehow expected Grazia to be genuinely delighted to see her again after so many years and easily able to soothe Emily's frayed nerves, particularly since she was the one who had always wanted Emily to come back to Italy in the first place. Grazia had given her the standard outward show of affection that was in her Italian nature to give, but, underneath it all, Emily could sense vexation.

"I had just arrived at the clinic today when… well, who do you think should turn up? The old lady herself!"

Grazia paused, her fork midway between her mouth and her plate and her face suddenly brightened by a loving look.

"Extraordinary, really, under the circumstances," she said. "Doesn't she blame you any more for her husband's death?"

Emily glanced across at the doctor with renewed interest.

"She must still have a little common sense then," said Grazia, "to realise that you couldn't defend him from a second heart attack. No amount of rich connections could help him there! Did she come to make amends to you?"

"To give me some of the insurance money, you mean?"

The doctor laughed viciously and Emily eyed him curiously. She did not like the look of this man with his neatly trimmed moustache and carefully brushed hair. He seemed conceited and she wondered what it was Grazia saw in him. A veneer of manners hardly seemed a good enough reason for someone falling in love with a man like that and Grazia did give the impression of a woman very much in love.

"Emily and I are going to visit the catacombs tomorrow;" said Grazia, pulling away from her lover and speaking in

English, perhaps trying to make up for her previous neglect of her guest. "Would you like to join us, Toni?"

"No, no," he said, glancing at Emily. "*Voi inglesi* love this *Roma antica, non è vero?*"

Emily raised her eyebrows at his scornful voice as well as his pronunciation of "love" to rhyme with "stove", wondering vaguely if what he said was supposed to be some sort of veiled criticism about her nation's characteristics; she said nothing. Instead, after a short awkward silence, she picked up the cheap plastic handbag that Grazia had already sneered at and told them she was going to the bathroom.

There, she was irked to notice that the hem of her long skirt was coming undone. She stared unhappily at her reflection in the full-length gilt mirror. Unsettled, anxious, desirous of she knew not what, worn out by the bitterness of being made redundant in London from a clerical job she had in any case hated, she wondered what had happened to her life as she fumbled in her bag for the bright pink lip gloss she had bought in the duty-free shop at Heathrow.

A couple of teenage girls with high-pitched, squeaking voices opened the door and broke her reflective mood. Catching sight of herself again in the mirror, she realised she could be the age of these chattering girls' mothers, and then, just as the door was swinging shut, they heard the sound of gunshot and shattering glass in the restaurant, immediately followed by the noise of people shouting and screaming. The girls became as pale as ghosts and looked at Emily as if an older woman would automatically be able to give them reassurance. She pretended to be calm and told them brusquely that there was bound to be a perfectly normal explanation and was therefore shocked to see Toni Cellamare lying in a pool of blood while Grazia, surrounded by a crowd of dimly discernible faces, knelt on the ground beside him, desperately screaming for an ambulance.

The proprietor, a plump Sicilian who seemed more concerned about the damage done to his windows, stood nearby, rocking backwards and forwards on his toes without any apparent sign of stress, as if such events were everyday occurrences in his restaurant, and ordered the panic-stricken young waiters in their evening dress to dig about in cupboards for more napkins so that Grazia could staunch the deep wound in Toni's shoulder.

When the police and ambulance finally arrived, Grazia was precise and succinct, a model of efficiency in such overwhelmingly dramatic circumstances. She had nothing to tell the police and declined going to the hospital with Toni. Her face wore a strange haunted look that Emily had never seen before as she now marched obsessively up and down in the practically deserted restaurant until turning on Emily with wild eyes.

"I saw him, the beast! Well, kind of saw him! Anyway, they'll think I'm a witness, won't they! They'll come after me too!"

Emily tried to calm her down with some soothing words that Grazia did not hear.

"Toni has done something illegal, I don't know exactly what but I'm afraid! There were these people who hung around the clinic. Toni didn't want me there, told me it wasn't any of my business… Foreign, I don't know, Romanians maybe or Russians. The tall thin one, with the terrible face – it could easily have been him on the motorbike tonight!"

Grazia paused for breath and leaned unsteadily against a table.

"Well, I hope he's not got himself mixed up in drugs! Anyway, why can't you tell the police all this?" asked Emily with the breezy logic of northern climes. "Set them on the trail of these people, I mean?"

Grazia turned on her viciously in the style of a dog baring its teeth.

"It's hardly as simple as that, is it?" Toni's up to his neck too… He would just end up getting arrested!"

She made Emily's head spin with tales of violent men and dark alleyways on the outskirts of town barely lit up by broken streetlamps. Their unfinished dinner seemed something very distant as all Grazia could now think of was the moment when Toni had slipped to the ground and her perfect world had fallen apart.

CHAPTER 2

FATHER AND SON

Emily was alone in the spare bedroom, staring bleakly at the discarded grey suit she had been wearing in the *Forchetta d'Oro* and thinking that its grey colour was exactly the same as poor Grazia's face had been earlier that evening in the restaurant and later too when they had driven back to the flat in Toni's car. Looking meaningfully at each other before saying goodnight, Grazia had opened her mouth as if to speak, whatever it was remaining on the tip of her tongue, unsaid. Emily was not good at offering words of comfort so she made no comment whatsoever and Grazia put her silence down to the proverbially cold nature of the English.

When Grazia phoned the hospital and finally managed to speak to an unhelpful receptionist, she was told, in a peremptory tone of voice, that Dr. Antonio Cellamare was still under the effect of the anaesthetic. With a sense of foreboding, the thought struck Grazia that perhaps she was being reckless to come back here where the hit man would surely know she lived with Toni. She remembered how she had woken up that morning with the enthusiasm the imminent arrival of any foreign guest aroused in her, to be quickly dispelled by the reality of Emily's intrusive presence. She could barely recall what else had happened that day. Only the sound of gunshot and the glimpse she had had of the killer's masked face had managed to penetrate her muddled thoughts.

What a joke it had been at first to have an affair with a man who dabbled in what she knew must be criminal activities. She had never inquired into what exactly were these Eastern European contacts he occasionally alluded to; all she knew was that she had never to mention them to anybody. Frankly, she had no desire to know more; she did not want her fragile illusions about her generous lover to be shattered by some painful unwelcome truth about just where he got all his money from.

When she appeared at the breakfast table the following morning, Grazia was dressed in a white silky shirt and tightly-belted, Giorgio Armani, suede trousers that somehow managed to make her feel better, in control of any situation. Having finally fallen asleep when the first pale light of dawn was already in the sky, she felt tired this morning as well as anxious. Emily looked guardedly at her, unable to read anything but steely resolution in Grazia's proud face. She felt thoroughly overwhelmed herself by the memory of their horrifically freakish evening and all its potential implications. All at once her own problems seemed quite petty in comparison.

Instinctively, Emily started to make herself look busy in Grazia's immaculate kitchen, making coffee and setting out matching green cups on the wipe clean tablecloth. Italian women rarely looked idle at home and Emily had quickly learned to adopt local habits.

"We have to get away from here," announced Grazia suddenly. "You know that, don't you? It's too dangerous now."

"Too dangerous?" echoed Emily blankly. "What do you mean? What about Toni?"

"Exactly the point I'm making. We have to get him out of that third-rate hospital."

"And how can we do that?" Emily asked.

"Oh, why is it that you English have no imagination? Everything is possible if you would only make it so. That's why you've managed to muck up your own life so horribly, Emily!"

Emily was taken aback by such undeserved vehemence and, after a short silence, Grazia apologised stiffly and settled down to her usual meagre breakfast – a thimbleful of espresso and one wafer-thin biscuit covered with a wafer-thin layer of strictly sugarless apricot jam.

The intercom squealed suddenly and Grazia turned anguished eyes towards the door. She was relieved to find out it was only her Costa Rican cleaning lady whom she had to tell, very curtly, to come back another day, another month, another year. She failed to pay any attention to Emily's own anxious expression, although she did notice, with a certain disdain, just how pale and dishevelled her guest was looking and thanked God with heartfelt gratitude for His having given her innate Italian style. Poor Emily after all. Perhaps if she had been more demanding of the people in her life, she might even have set her life back on the right track. She should have married that rich fiancé of hers when she still had the chance and that was for sure. Grazia was still musing over this consideration when Emily blurted out with unusual verve:

"What about your boyfriend then? What exactly has he been getting involved in?"

Grazia assumed a mask of studied indifference.

"Well, what an extraordinary tone of voice coming from you, I must say! I don't see that it's any business of yours either."

Emily immediately looked sheepish and Grazia continued.

"OK, let's say he's acted in a less than legal way, but that's not the point now, is it! We have a problem at hand and we have to resolve it. I certainly have no intention of shutting myself up here!"

"But you said you had to get away fast. Doesn't that mean you're running away from the problem?"

Grazia had a very sharp tongue when she wanted and she felt like using it now on Emily. Instead, she banged the metallic coffee pot on to the table and began to wave her hands about in agitation.

"What can you ever understand!" she shouted. "Quite nothing!"

After this outburst Grazia fell silent and sat hunched at the table, her arms clutched protectively around her body. She gazed, in apparent wonder, at the diamond ring on her finger that Toni had given her as a pledge of his love.

"Of course I'm angry with Toni," Grazia half-whispered. "But I don't want to lose him, can you understand that?"

She stared at Emily with wide apart, frightened eyes, craving her reassurance and receiving it wholeheartedly. Emily was watching Grazia gazing out of the window, with a frown on her face. The flat, in an upmarket residential area dotted with foreign embassies, was on the fourth floor and Emily wondered if Grazia could possibly be thinking of doing something silly. All the result of getting mixed up with sinister men like Toni Cellamare, Emily thought primly to herself as her attention was caught by the incongruous sight of a holy picture on the wall above the television – the gory martyrdom of some long-haired tattered saint.

At about the same time, Francesco Cellamare was staring at a Rembrandt print of a sullen-looking man in a shiny cuirass. The nurse kept glancing surreptitiously at the young novice priest with the fine profile and glossy black hair that shone just like the sable coat her dull dentist husband had given her at Christmas. What made such a handsome man become a priest, she wondered. He was not even emaciated or pale as she would have expected someone with a vocation in that line to be but broad-shouldered and olive-skinned in the best Mediterranean tradition. Perhaps sensing her scrutiny, he turned around to glance in her direction and she began to busy herself with patients' files.

Scorn or incredulity was what Francesco half-expected from people his own age, certainly not admiration for his good looks. As a matter of fact, his own father would have much preferred it if he had in fact followed the path of loose-living youth rather than that of religious fervour and Francesco had had to get used to his jibes as well. At school, Francesco had been religious-minded, too much so for his boisterous companions who had teased him without mercy. Unhappy at school, the summer holidays could never come fast enough for Francesco's liking because it meant going to stay with the *contadini* on his mother's small property in the heart of Umbria. How he had loved Signor Rosati and his good-natured wife, perhaps more than he loved his own father. Their son Giorgio had become his very dear friend in spite of his ignorance and simplicity, or perhaps because of it. His more sophisticated friends in Rome would have considered Giorgio a complete country bumpkin. When they returned from their summer holidays, they boasted about Mediterranean cruises or expensive summer schools in Britain or America. Francesco had no such pretensions even when he was finally obliged to go to a summer school in Cambridge one year, enjoying the experience rather against all his expectations. If he had been asked to choose a place to go on holiday, he would have chosen the farmhouse in Umbria and the Rosati household. They went to church together every Sunday morning. The small congregation gathered outside the church to speak to Don Carlo who knew everything there was to know about his parishioners. Francesco began to talk to him about his faith and his ideals and, suddenly, as they talked, his doubts vanished and he knew he had a vocation for the Church.

On his eighteenth birthday, hugging the doorway of his father's study as if exhorting courage from the very jambs themselves, the dreaded moment had come to inform his father of his momentous decision. His father had glared at him, a gloomy sigh punctuating the silence. It was never going to be the right moment to tell him in any case. Dr. Cellamare accused his only son of being *difficile* and *un perfetto imbecille* while Francesco hugged the doorway a little more. In those far-off days, he used to have a heavy fringe shadowing his face so he peeped out at his father from an awkward angle, something that managed to annoy his scowling parent even more. Dr. Cellamare had already imagined his intellectual son studying architecture and pursuing an illustrious career designing classically-inspired structures. He considered himself quite the art lover as well as collector and would have much preferred the study of Greek caryatids to medicine. But his own father, the stern son of poverty-stricken southern peasants, had wanted his clever son to become a doctor and that had been the end of the matter.

Francesco had never got on with his father. He disapproved of his father's affairs, barely concealed before his beloved mother's untimely illness and untimely death as well as after. His sister had reacted in an entirely different manner. She had taken to rebelling, dropping out of university to go off to London with one of her boyfriends, much to the horror of Toni Cellamare. His daughter had been so rude and unsettled of late that he had kept quiet even when he finally made this taciturn boyfriend's acquaintance. Toni could not see what Chiara could ever find attractive in that charmless, uncouth individual. As for Francesco, he had fervently hoped that his son's "vocation" was just a passing fancy, something he would have grown out of, like getting fed up with tennis lessons. An overly rigorous Jesuit schooling in his own very distant youth had turned him away from anybody remotely resembling a priest. As far as he was concerned, this notion of Francesco's must have come on very suddenly and would eventually disappear with the same speed.

Francesco Cellamare waited patiently for his father to regain consciousness. He passed the time perusing leaflets that seemed mainly to deal with urinary problems and erectile dysfunction. A door opened quietly and a middle-aged woman in a white coat, presumably the doctor, came out and exchanged a look with him that meant he could finally go inside.

There was a dull silence in the room, broken only by the sound of the patient's laboured breathing.

"I've kept you waiting," said Dr. Cellamare in a wry tone of voice.

It was immediately obvious that it was painful when he spoke. Nothing could usually stop him from making long monologues, particularly where his son's unfortunate career choices were concerned. Francesco came up to the bed and looked as if he wanted to kiss his father's cheek.

"*Ragazzo mio*, you're very quiet!"

He groaned softly and paused to take a deep ragged breath, dismayed as always at the sight of his son's long black cassock and the dark, curly hair he had somehow managed to comb in such a way that it reminded Toni of a skullcap. Francesco was stroking his father's hand, the palm of which seemed strangely clammy to the touch until he took his hand away to switch on the bedside light. He was appalled to see his father like this. It was as if he had aged, virtually overnight, his haggard, other-worldly face a ghastly grey colour that Francesco had never seen before. Hesitantly, he held out a little bundle.

"I got you some of your favourite chocolates."

Francesco rubbed at his chin as he held them out to his father who clutched the beribboned box with one hand and smiled at long last.

Toni Cellamare would recover then. His son, head bowed in recognition and humble gratefulness, murmured a silent prayer to a roughly-hewn clay Madonna above the bed.

"I suppose the police will want to speak to you? I still can't understand why anyone should want to shoot you? It's completely crazy!"

Francesco had been speechless when Grazia had telephoned him with the news. It had seemed like a scene from one of those detective stories written by the American authors his mother had liked so much. Grazia said she knew nothing else and added that she had been unable to get a good look at the would-be assassin's face. Francesco had felt that incipient fear he had felt as a child playing blind man's bluff, unable to find anyone, the din of children's voices nearby only managing to frustrate and upset him.

"Francesco *mio*, you have to help me get away at once. I'm not going to stay here."

Last night Toni Cellamare had looked Death in the face, crawling about on his hands and knees before falling on to the floor in a bloody heap at Grazia's feet. Recovering consciousness in the hospital, he had immediately been assailed by terror, not only at the thought that a would-be assassin might very likely strike again, but that his own personal demons could be catching up with him at long last. He began to sweat once more at the very thought, as if the air-conditioned hospital had suddenly turned into a torrid hothouse. He could well imagine who wanted to see him dead and he would have instinctively shouted out their names but for the fact that it was out of the question – things had to remain secret at all costs. Now he had to get up and out of here. He could already imagine people in the adjacent rooms eavesdropping on his conversations, apart from him hating the thought of lying here for much longer in this pokey little room, a sitting duck.

"Don't we have to wait until they think you can go home? Look, I can speak to the doctor of course but, I mean, you have just undergone surgery, *papà*."

"No, that's quite out of the question. Get me out of here now! It's not safe, I tell you! I must get away from here!"

Francesco looked baffled.

"Tell the police whatever it is that's bothering you so much. What on earth's stopping you?"

"No, I said no police. Just get me out of here now!"

CHAPTER 3

THE HOUSE IN THE HILLS

So it was that, one fine day, Emily and Grazia came to be perusing the disused hayloft of a dilapidated old farmhouse in hills that were well over two hundred kilometres south of Rome. Grazia was still trying to banish thoughts of guns and violent murderers from her mind, thoughts that had managed to keep her awake every night. She unstuck the unyielding rusty bolt with all her might and they went on up rickety wooden steps that creaked loudly under their every step. Emily asked her where the light switch was, quite oblivious to the turmoil that was thrashing itself out in the other woman's mind. Grazia's face had assumed such a steely mask recently that it was practically impossible to surmise anything about what was going on inside her head. She flicked on a plastic lighter, revealing a pokey loft that contained an assortment of sundry objects: faded lampshades here, some filthy crumpled tarpaulins there, all smelling vaguely and not at all unpleasantly of damp firewood. The house itself, once they managed to fit the key into the lock, was cramped and badly-furnished. It had belonged to Toni's father and left practically to rack and ruin when he had died. Underneath the loft, there was a kind of byre where, by the look of the metallic rings on the walls, sheep or cattle had once been kept.

"What do you think of this peculiar place then?" asked Emily in a light-hearted tone of voice.

She was feeling a kind of childlike excitement, as if she were in the thralls of an adventure. Grazia stood hunched in her solitary corner, looking glum, while Emily chattered on like a schoolgirl.

"When do you think they'll arrive?" she asked Grazia, suddenly feeling a little guilty about her own elated mood.

"I've no idea."

"If you'd like to talk things over…"

"No."

Emily left her alone after that. She was listening to the faint pealing of church bells in the distance and she breathed in the fresh tangy air outside with satisfaction. She had been away from the countryside for far too long. This was life, she thought, not Rome or Glasgow or London – least of all, London. A temping job came to mind, where she had had to work in a dingy basement, the electric light constantly switched on because the pallid northern sunlight never managed to filter its way through the grimy panes.

Grazia glanced anxiously about her. Before they left Rome, she had kept imagining gunmen ducking around a variety of corners. She had begun to dread going out of her house, the very thought of doing so making her feel faint. She would peer out through a slit in the kitchen curtains, expecting to see suspicious-looking men hanging around her car, still parked outside in the street. The very day they left she had seen somebody clasping something in his hand and looking up at her window. She had resolutely closed all of the shutters, to the bemusement of Emily, who had been hemming a skirt in the waning light. She said nothing, however, since Grazia had that quarrelsome look on her face again. She had tried teasing her once about her jumpiness but Grazia had sworn at her with the eloquence that only Italian swearwords could manage to express and they had both been left feeling breathless. Departing from the city in a great hurry, Grazia had been constantly looking backwards in her rear screen mirror. The usual chaotic Roman traffic had left Emily feeling relieved to be finally putting the labyrinthine streets and the crowds of faceless people behind her.

Standing outside now, the pair of them were both following the flight of a solitary eagle across the sky when the sound of a car broke the spell of their meditative silence. Dr. Cellamare's Alfa Romeo made a tremendous clatter on the uneven flagstones, scattering great black, clamorous crows in its wake. Emily was curious to see a handsome young man, dressed in very sombre clothes, come out from the door of the driver's seat.

Grazia was pressing Toni's hands to her own and looking at him with heartfelt relief.

"We had to dodge the hospital security guards. It was harder than I thought it would be but here I am at long last," he said, shaking his head slowly as he stroked her long dark hair.

Toni did not bother to introduce his son to the English woman; he had in fact barely noticed her and Emily just assumed he was somebody who had been hired to drive the car. Dr. Cellamare's face had assumed a completely different expression from that ill-fated evening at the restaurant. She could hardly recognise him. Suffering was stamped on his prominent features and she noticed deep furrowed lines on his forehead for the very first time.

They were just going into the house when he suddenly turned around and looked at Emily.

"Oh, of course, excuse me for my rudeness," he began in his hesitant English before quickly reverting to Italian. "This is my son, Francesco, or should I say, Don Francesco."

Emily could not help exchanging a questioning glance with Grazia when she heard the word *Don*.

"I'm pleased to meet you," said the young priest in perfect English. "I like Britain very much, you know. I visited

25

Cambridge when I was younger – all that greenery and the students on the river rowing their…"

"Punts?" she suggested helpfully.

He continued speaking enthusiastically about the splendours of Cambridge and Grazia took this as an opportunity to take piles of shopping out of the car and to arrange everything with loud thuds on the kitchen shelves. They ate *prosciutto* sandwiches and had coffee in little chipped cups, with Emily being amazed, as usual, by how they always claimed to be restored by such a tiny cupful of strong, syrupy *espresso*. Grazia cleared away the cups before Emily had even finished and began cleaning things up with an energetic fury certainly not well received by the dripping tap, a stern expression stamped on her face. Her lovely black hair rippled down her back with every single sinuous movement and Toni glanced at her appreciatively from time to time. Emily looked out of the kitchen window that overlooked the darkening hillside. It would take her some time to get used to its silence after the din of the city. The sky had turned a deep gentian violet colour and a breeze from the open window ruffled her hair, carrying with it the promise of profound dreamy night.

She was brought rudely down to earth by the thud of Toni Cellamare's heavy black briefcase on the table where she was still sitting.

"May I?" he said, continuing to hover in front of her. "I would like to do a little studying here and since this is the only place…"

Emily smiled a little awkwardly.

"Oh, certainly, don't let me get in your way."

Francesco sat down at the table beside his father and took out a thick-lined notebook.

Emily went along to her tiny bedroom. Quaintly dilapidated, she reassured herself, gazing at the peeling plaster and the windowpane that gaped an inch at the bottom before she had even opened it. She wondered who it was had slept in this bedroom such a long time ago. An empty wooden shelf went all around the walls, serving no apparent purpose. Her room was immediately above the front door and she looked out on to the silent courtyard. The valley they had driven through, densely covered with oaks and beeches, was full of such farmhouses, deserted by poor southern farmers who had emigrated, very often across the ocean, in the hope of finding a better life. Grazia had told her their nearest neighbours were likely going to be those of the Santa Chiara convent, at least a kilometre away over the hillside. Emily had been quite looking forward to the sight of wimples and grey habits in such a setting but there had as yet been no glimpse of any nuns. She began musing over the fact that a sinister man with mysterious activities like Toni Cellamare should have a priest for a son, and such a very handsome one at that.

Was it her imagination or had Toni Cellamare looked at her with vaguely malicious eyes? He always seemed to be giving her sidelong glances for no particular reason.

She undressed quickly and stretched herself out on the narrow bed that she had made up with the perfectly laundered sheets they had brought from Rome and fell asleep, still wondering what it was that had made Grazia fall in love with him.

In an upstairs room at that very moment, Grazia and Toni were on the verge of an argument. She had a vicious expression on her face, as if poised to strike. She had just finished sorting his bandages when he began to speak, very disparagingly, about Emily.

"You told me the *testa di cazzo* was just a temporary visitor to Rome. Why is she here?"

"I'd like to know what you've got against her. She's perfectly harmless and means well. She's kept me sane these last few days while I've been worrying myself to death."

"You!" exclaimed Toni. "Why should you worry? It's my skin they're after, not yours!

"What have you told your son exactly?" she asked in a quieter voice, as if suddenly fearful the walls might be listening.

"Nothing whatsoever. He'd just go running to the police and spill the beans, so he's not to be trusted. His bloody conscience would bother him! I should send him to hell, what with all this damned priest business!"

"Oh, I wouldn't worry about that. He could still change his mind and, anyway, there's always Chiara to give you your grandchildren if that's what you're worried about!"

Toni's face darkened and she began to laugh.

"Oh yes, but her children won't have your precious surname, I forgot! Well then, you'll just have to throw some temptation in Francesco's way…"

"That's it!" he cried excitedly. "At least your snooty English friend can be good for something. English girls were always considered the easiest lay when I spent my summers in Rimini!"

Grazia looked scandalised.

"You will fuckin' not! She's been having a hard time recently and, anyway, she's not that kind of girl!"

"Oh yes, the same old story – and then she just happened to come to Italy looking for consolation, did she? She must have some experience, surely, or has she spent her entire life in a cloister?"

Grazia had begun to undress, carefully draping her clothes over a couple of chairs. Toni lay back on the pillows and watched her. Something about the way she moved had made him change his tone of voice to mutter the same old love-lies that Grazia had heard a hundred times before. She still fell for it every time. He knew how to play on her vanity par excellence and she was quickly lured into bed, momentarily forgetful of the anxiety this present situation inspired in her.

She tucked herself up under the sheets where he made love to her with rude passion. He was quick, selfish and she regretted having given into him so quickly. He must have sensed her anger and began speaking quietly to her in what he imagined was a soothing tone of voice but sounding so horribly pleased with himself that she got even crosser. She turned over on her side and switched off the bedside light with a curt *buona notte*.

Beside her, Toni lay quietly, aware that he had been at fault. There was no need for all that gruffness though. After all he had been through, he was lucky to be alive. Grazia should make herself more amenable – these were critical times for them both and it would certainly not do for her to turn against him now that she already knew far too much about his illegal activities.

Many years before, he had acquired a taste for money and had begun spending more than he should. Grazia, from this point of view, had been a godsend. She was by nature thrifty, practical, and sensible, just like all her good Lombard forebears before her, and did her best to wean him away from his expensive tastes in flashy sports cars and his constant desire for showy extravagance. Indeed, this age-old desire of his must have abated somewhat or he would not now be staying in this old hovel, with the plaster peeling off the ceiling.

He felt Grazia moving about in the bed. He looked at her and saw that her eyes were sparkling in the half-light that filtered in through the unshuttered windows. Her tears fell thick and fast, while he remained motionless in the bed, musing over their very first meeting, the happy moments and exotic locations they had enjoyed together. Why did she always have to end up crying? He said nothing whatsoever and she was left feeling sad and irritated by his apparent insensitivity.

CHAPTER 4

HOMECOMING

"I can't stand the cheek of that daughter of yours! She wouldn't know what courtesy was, even if it slapped her in the face!"

Grazia spoke quickly and angrily, waking up Emily, who was unused to hearing people yell and shout. The Englishwoman cast a glance at the weather outside; sunny blue sky, summer in the air, a flock of sheep grazing on the distant hillside and a solitary eagle circling overhead, perhaps the very same one as the day before.

"Who does she think she is, judging me! She should pay more attention to her own behaviour, that's what I say, jumping from one bed to the next, anything for a quick lay!"

The echoing sound of shocked silence reverberated through the house, not so much the reaction of a father but that of the young priest. Grazia was referring, after all, to his sister.

Emily sat on the edge of her bed, hesitantly wondering whether it was an opportune moment to make an appearance in the kitchen and feeling rather like an awkward boarder on her first day at school. When she eventually plucked up enough courage to venture downstairs, Grazia was still bawling and gesticulating wildly. Emily exchanged rapid glances with Francesco over by the window; evidently, they felt mutually ill-at-ease. Toni Cellamare sulked and occasionally uttered an inept phrase that did nothing to placate Grazia, beside herself with fury. Emily was looking at Francesco, somehow expecting wisdom to issue forth from a priest. Instead, he seemed as embarrassed as she was, a fact he tried to hide behind a watery smile.

"You never see what's under your own nose, Toni! Chiara is just using you yet again, *vecchio imbecille!*"

Grazia poured forth another torrent of swearwords that were chillingly frank about Chiara's promiscuous nature. Toni looked taken aback by this shower of *"puttana"* and *"stronza"* and the sound of a car on the gravel was greeted practically with them all rejoicing apart from Grazia herself. Suddenly a young man with a gruff manner and a very pretty girl were adding to the general confusion in the small kitchen. Grazia's face assumed a mask of hollow pleasantness and her tormented trumpeting of two minutes before vanished mysteriously into thin air. They were introduced to Emily as Chiara Cellamare and Ricky Brown, her Irish boyfriend. Chiara was wearing a shimmering purple blouse and was heavily made-up, her thick black hair tied back in a sleek ponytail. In complete contrast to her, the young man was pale and colourless apart from a lurid yellow shirt that did not suit him at all and painfully short spiky hair that gave him the vague appearance of being an escaped convict; at the very least, he gave the impression of being filled with inner torment, someone struggling under the yoke of God only knew what. This first impression rather faded when he began to speak in a dull bored voice that gave an impression of rudeness. Toni Cellamare glared at him reproachfully all the while as Chiara smiled cheerfully, blissfully oblivious to any ill-feeling. It was not only the fact that Toni felt that this uncouth young man was unworthy of his beautiful daughter. Ricky Brown had been born into a staunch Protestant family, imbued from an early age with rancour against any form of

Catholicism. He begrudged Chiara her Catholic upbringing, lax enough as it had been and inexistent now and he could barely bring himself to speak civilly to that priestly brother of hers.

To his utter disdain, Toni noticed that Ricky and Emily had seized instinctively upon one another and were now chattering together in English in a corner of the kitchen. Ricky had managed to unwind and now had a tendency to gesticulate in the Italian fashion as well as standing too close to Emily for her liking. Occasionally, he would flash a lopsided grin at her that revealed a front tooth that was a little cracked. Their conversation was banal enough and one-sided – just a straightforward, rather tiresome account of the reason why he now found himself in Italy. He told her, in a grave tone of voice, that he was an animal rights activist, much concerned about the appalling way in which Italians treated their hunting dogs.

"They tie them up for most of the year on infernal chains a metre long," he said.

Hunting of any kind upset him.

"They shoot at innocent little birds anywhere they can. They're considered a delicacy here." Ricky paused and took a better look at Emily. "What did you say your name was? Oh yes, Emily, good name. Like my Aunt Emily May in Portrush – great place for holidays. Have you ever been there?"

Emily shook her head. Apart from that, she learned he had been working one summer for a publishing company in Rome, where he was supposed to have been selling educational English books to the innumerable private language schools there; he had met Chiara and they had gone back to London very soon after, where their relationship seemed to have become his whole occupation. Emily glanced surreptitiously at Chiara, now talking to her family in animated tones. Even Grazia was smiling in spite of her former vociferous objections to the girl. Then Toni Cellamare began holding forth about the current government as well as making rash assertions about Silvio Berlusconi's pristine honesty. As far as he was concerned, communists as well as Italian judges ought all to be shot. His relations stared at him in incredulous horror.

"*Dio mio, papà*," exclaimed Chiara. "I didn't realise you'd become so narrow-minded! I'm not going to stay here and listen to this kind of talk. Let's go away, Ricky!"

Her father's face immediately transformed itself into a mask of fawning smiles and he tried to win her over with a hundred and one excuses.

"It's not my fault, I tell you! I hear my staff speak in this way. Intolerance is so rife and Italy is going to the dogs!"

Francesco looked pensive and bit his lip. What was it that his father had been up to in any case? He was inclined to believe his father and a host of like-minded colleagues in the clinic where he operated might well be mixed up in some very dubious dealings. He could remember a strange incident there one day when he had arrived unexpectedly to find his father in deep conversation with two men and a woman. Their behaviour had immediately given him the impression that they were not patients. The woman had been wearing a bright red coat and had highly artificial blonde hair that only served to set off the many wrinkles in her suntanned face. She was putting something away in her expensive designer handbag, snapping it shut with one swift movement. Speaking coarsely in dialect to the older man, she stood up as soon as Francesco came in, signalling to the other to do the same. They were going out without a backward glance until the man, speaking in a threatening tone of voice, had suddenly turned around and said, "We'll square things up with you later. Make no mistake this time, I mean what I say!"

Francesco had not given too much thought to the pair until someone had tried to kill his father. The day before that fateful evening, he had gone to visit his father in the clinic and had found him surrounded by boxes filled with files. "Just tidying up," he had told Francesco, sending him on his way with some excuse or other.

Francesco had not yet confided any of this in Chiara, who had changed too much since she had become involved with her Irishman. He was vaguely aware that Ricky did not like him. He had, however, not yet quite fathomed the full extent of his rancour – Ricky kept insults unsaid and would only tease Chiara occasionally about the fact it was odd that brother and sister should be so different: one so holy, the other so profane. Chiara's family tried to meddle too much in Chiara's life, that was for sure, but that was Italian families for you. How he loved it now when she made fun of her doting parent behind his back, but then she would go and link her arm in her father's, caressing his cheek, something that always managed to irritate Ricky. What was the need for all these physical displays of affection? Ricky's own mother had never once hugged him, even when he had been an angel-faced little schoolboy. He knew nothing at all about Chiara's relationship or, rather, lack of it with her mother, who had only had eyes for darling Francesco, her pious son, and had never had any time for Chiara with her strange rebellious ways. Chiara could come home with cropped peroxide hair and an earring in her nose and her mother, already ailing and housebound, would barely look up from the book she was reading. Fortunately, Chiara had never heard what her mother said about her to Toni behind her back, that she was a troublemaker. Toni Cellamare had always defended his daughter from any form of criticism, always held her close. Chiara only had to lift a finger and she could get anything she wanted from her doting father.

Nobody mentioned her mother now, not even Francesco who had been so close to her. Their mother's house in Umbria, where Francesco had spent such happy summers, had been sold off with what now seemed indecent haste. Chiara had in any case already managed to squander any inheritance Signora Cellamare had left her, instead of hoarding it the way Francesco seemed to do, and had now come back to her father, shored up in these remote hills, far from any living soul. She rather liked this old house that she only vaguely remembered from one brief childhood visit and that seemed enormous after the two-roomed flat where she had been living with Ricky.

In the days to follow, she would take walks to the little nearby lake with Ricky. The weather was already warm and summer had arrived ahead of time. The two of them went out on the trusty moped that Ricky had managed to repair and did the shopping in the little village that overlooked the lake. Grazia cooked the food for everybody and refused point-blank anyone's assistance in the kitchen; she could be heard shouting sometimes at poor Emily, who would only be wanting to make herself a cup of tea from a stash of teabags she appeared to keep stowed away in an ugly plastic handbag. Toni, meanwhile, was getting ever more tense and irritable, parading around the house as if expecting the siege of Leningrad. Sometimes, Francesco would come and take his place at the window, as if they really had arranged a watch and would stare, motionless, at the flickering shadows that danced in the bushes, quite unlike his usual self. Chiara noticed none of this. She was too busy roaming the countryside with Ricky, avoiding Grazia in the kitchen; she would only be scrubbing old cupboards or making focaccia that could easily be bought in the village, a glum expression stamped on her face, bustling about from morning to night in tasks that presumably gave some sort of self-imposed order to her day. Chiara was enjoying delaying her return to Rome indefinitely. Engulfed as he was by his private worries and continually niggling at anybody who would listen to him, her father became a secondary concern for the moment as she and Ricky enjoyed the kind of prolonged honeymoon that had, for any number of reasons, always been impossible in Rome or London.

CHAPTER 5

THE SHOTGUN

The days passed without any of this ill-assorted group realising that time was slipping away at the old farmhouse in the Apulian hills. The countryside was marvellous at that time of year. Emily happily wandered around the woods, gathering wild berries in a wicker basket she had found in a cupboard. Grazia was the only one who paid any attention to her appearance, powdering her nose at regular intervals and applying her Estee Lauder lipstick as she cleaned the kitchen with obsessive energy and fought a never-ending battle with colonies of ants. Chiara and Ricky would just fling on their clothes in the morning and run outside eagerly, Chiara trampling the long grass and pulling Ricky along behind her as she shrieked in merriment like an over-excited child. He just wanted to "relax"– the word he uttered constantly while playing with the straps of Chiara's skimpy tops. No one could ever have imagined danger lurking in that charming corner of paradise, not even Toni Cellamare, who was finally starting to unwind and even to smile again, revealing teeth that were nicotine-stained and irregular. Sometimes, Francesco would make a half-hearted attempt to speak to him about what had happened at the restaurant, still trying to give an identity to the gunman who had got away, but his father would only look confused and helpless as if it were all a faraway event, something that had happened to someone else.

Francesco probed his father gently, trying to discover something about the events leading up to his attempted murder. He was convinced the band or whoever it had been was still at large, as convinced in fact as Toni Cellamare himself was, even if he did his best not to let anyone know his thoughts about the whole matter. Neither did he confide in Grazia. For now, he felt safe enough, shored-up in the isolated farmhouse and began to retreat into a fantasy world of his own. He had discovered a box of model soldiers in the attic and spent the mornings laying them out on the floor in what had once been the dining room. He even sent Chiara down to the nearest village to search for enamel paint to touch up his halberdiers so that they would shine in the artificial light of the north-facing room.

"What on earth are you doing, *papà*?" asked Francesco one day.

Toni looked up from his endeavours, bent over the table, and replied with a boyish grin.

"I have spies gathering information from the other side."

It was all too much for Francesco who took to his heels and headed back to Rome for a while. He came back towards the end of July when the awful crush of tourists around the Vatican had begun to depress him. He hated crowds. Now he found his father with an old model train set, tooting away with a tin whistle while the trains sped around the circular track, a gang of bandits from the Wild West wanting to rob the train and the sheriff with his posse trying to stop them. However, it was when his father changed tack all of a sudden and began uprooting the paving stones around the house that Francesco decided it was once more high time he returned to the hustle and bustle of tourist crowds in Rome. Toni Cellamare was by now convinced there was a secret passageway under the house. He would crouch down to listen to the ground, then he would wander around the house, huddling in odd corners and tapping the ground, convinced he was going to find a secret passageway that led out from the house. He would go upstairs to look outside from the tiny garret window that overlooked the front courtyard. He climbed up on to large chests to seize hold of inexplicably-placed hooks, imagining they might be the very levers that would open up the walls. Grazia found her neat and tidy kitchen cupboards being turned upside-down and only managed to get rid of him by throwing a metal sieve at his head one day.

Munching sunflower seeds one after the other, Toni went to stand like a sentinel at the windowsill where Grazia kept her pots of mint and basil. Grazia was in fact more than fed-up, cooped-up in their hillside prison, and was irritable with everybody. Then there was the sight of Chiara and Ricky wandering barefoot through the dry grass, hand-in-hand, completely oblivious to the external world. Grazia would watch them out of the kitchen window and note the way Ricky's lanky figure and wide shoulders continually brushed against Chiara as they walked.

One day, towards the end of July, Grazia had just turned away from the window and was busy stoking up the embers of a rusty old barbecue as well as poking at sausages on the grill. Emily was in the kitchen too, messing around with a bag of flour. She would insist on making fruitcakes and leaving a mess, irritating Grazia because she always took such a long time to tidy up and put things away in the right place.

"I went down to the village today," said Emily slowly, hesitantly, in that infuriating way she had. "There was an accident at the crossroads into the main street. A crowd of people round a boy with a moped, lying on the ground."

"Did you stop to take a look?"

"Oh no, I didn't want to. I didn't want to risk being noticed either."

Emily had made an unpleasant discovery herself, that Toni Cellamare's farmhouse was not nearly as inconspicuous as he liked to make out - she had looked up towards their sloping hillside and had noticed its bright terracotta roof standing out for miles around. The crowd standing around the boy on the ground had noticed her too, she was sure, and had perhaps begun to wonder about this stranger in their midst. They stared at her with ill-feeling in their ruddy, weather-beaten faces.

Emily was beginning to wonder why she was here at all and having to put up with any hardship whatsoever for Toni's sake. She was tiring of the tumbledown house with its peeling plaster and rickety old furniture. Emily shook out the tablecloth Grazia had given her, scattering crumbs on the grassy verge at the back of the house, apparently the only place that was deemed acceptable for this purpose. She gazed gloomily at the stagnant water that lay inside the unused dogs' bowls and tried to imagine Toni Cellamare as a little boy in this same house, going to school presumably in this small village. The people here would surely still remember him and this house too. The crowd at the roadside had unnerved her today. They had made her feel even more like a foreigner, with their staring eyes and low whispering. Then when she came back here, she had to put up with Grazia's short temper and sharp tongue. As far as she was concerned, Emily was not even able to fold a napkin adequately. The fresh milk she had bought in the village had somehow gone sour in the heat of the car on the way home and Grazia had mumbled some expletive or other in Emily's direction. The atmosphere hung heavy with the feel of an impending argument. The bar of plain chocolate Emily had bought for Grazia in the village shop had not melted, miraculously enough, and she now propped it up against Grazia's jars of homemade fig jam.

Suddenly, a single loud shot resounded through the wood, followed by the din made by flocks of birds rising above the trees in desperate flight. Outside the kitchen, Toni was peering through a narrow opening in the front door. Fear blocked him on the threshold and caused him untold anguish just as Grazia ran out to him.

"Well, what are you doing here? Go upstairs and lock yourself in the bedroom. I'll see what that sound was."

"You're going outside?" asked Emily incredulously, real concern in her voice.

"There's nothing like a confrontation, is there!" said Grazia triumphantly.

She pulled a knife out from the kitchen drawer and smiled at the horrified expression on Emily's face.

"Oh, no need to look like that – it's far too blunt to inflict any damage!"

She pushed past Toni.

"I can't stand this inaction," she said. "We have to do something!"

Toni immediately covered his face with his hands and huddled into a corner behind the door.

Sparrows in front of the house scattered quickly at Grazia's approach.

"Come out, come out, whoever you are!" she cried into the trees, presumably trying to provoke a response from whoever had fired the shotgun. "I don't care a damn about your threats, do you hear me?"

Her eyes were squinting in the sunlight, giving her face a scornful expression just as an old man with white hair, double-barreled shotgun draped casually over one shoulder, appeared out of the trees. He was tutting loudly and looked very put out by the sound of Grazia's shouting.

"What's all the noise about? Who were you expecting anyway? I hope you haven't gone and rung the police now?"

"Who are you?" asked Grazia, brought up short at the sight of such an innocuous-looking figure.

"Giocondo's the name, Pino Giocondo."

A black dog came running out of the wood, between its teeth a bird that it dropped gently at the old man's feet. It made a little howling sound and looked up at its master's face in abject adoration. Pino Giocondo leant over and patted the dog that now leapt up and down excitedly before bouncing off once more.

"Oh, that's a terrible dog I have there. Far too young for an old man like myself. I'm hardly able to keep up with him!" He paused to glance sheepishly at Grazia. "Well, I hope you'll not mind this little mistake of mine, this wandering into your neck of the woods, I mean?"

Grazia did not reply immediately; she was still feeling disconcerted by the discovery that the man who had fired the shot was not the evil criminal she had been imagining.

She countered his question with one of her own.

"Nobody ever comes up here. Is this the first time you've shot in these woods?"

The old man moved his weight from one foot to the other and frowned.

"I won't pass by this way another time, that's for sure," he said, evidently thinking that this was answer enough.

"Ask him why he hunts at all," said Emily, who had come out of the house by this time and found the old man's dialect very difficult to understand. "Poor little birds!"

Grazia glanced contemptuously at her. Emily persevered in an albeit fainter voice.

"Why does he have to shoot birds?"

Of course Pino Giocondo could not understand Italian very well when it was spoken in such a strange foreign accent. He looked appraisingly at these two women, so out of place in this remote setting.

"Well, I'll be getting along then," he said, pointing upwards at the sky. "There's maybe a storm brewing over there. We'll have rain tonight."

He nodded at them and disappeared again into the woods, leaving the two women staring after him.

41

Grazia turned steely eyes on Emily.

"Why do you want to make such a fuss? He only shot a few birds, for God's sake, birds he'll take home with him and eat. What's wrong with that?"

Her outburst silenced whatever Emily had been about to say on the matter of poaching.

"Toni! You can come out now! The coast's clear!" announced Grazia ironically. "You can continue demolishing the paving-stones outside if you want to!"

Nobody answered and Grazia went inside the house again.

"The bandit's gone away! You can come out from your hidey-hole!"

Toni reappeared at last, dressed up as some kind of mountaineer, to Grazia's utter amazement – heavy hiking boots, ribbed pullover in spite of the heat and a shotgun draped carelessly over his shoulder as if he had been carrying one all his life, Grazia stopped short at the sight of him.

"And where the hell have you been keeping that, I'd like to know?" she exclaimed.

He looked down at the gun as if he was seeing it for the first time. The way he was holding it so tightly made Emily reflect ominously upon the serried ranks of tin soldiers that Toni had amassed upstairs and wonder if he was not simply going out of his mind.

"Go ahead, shoot us all!" continued Grazia in an indescribably anguished tone of voice.

He tossed the gun over his other shoulder and looked her straight in the eye.

"Isn't it you who always keeps telling me I shouldn't run away? They wanted to kill me, don't you remember? They'd have killed me if I… hadn't run away! But I can't run away forever, can I? Look at me, Grazia, can I hide forever?"

He looked so crushed and crestfallen that Grazia went up to him and put her arms around him.

42

"Oh, Toni, things will work out somehow. This is only an interlude, an unfortunate interlude."

She gazed at him fondly and the distressed expression on his face slowly disappeared.

"I believe you, Grazia," he said, a boyish grin suddenly making him look years younger. "I thought you might have felt you were wasting your time here with me."

"Oh, I'm doing my best not to waste my time. I'm always busy, haven't you noticed, Toni?" She threw her long dark hair over her shoulders in what was a charmingly feminine gesture. "After all, we're only a stone's throw away from civilisation really – that's what I tell myself – we can go back whenever we like."

"Like tomorrow," he said.

"Tomorrow – no, it's too soon."

Grazia pursed her lips and pressed her fingertips together, glancing back at Emily as if seeking reassurance.

"We're having a kind of holiday here," she said. "What's wrong with that?"

Toni looked out of the window, a distant look in his sorrowful dark eyes. His index finger was drawing a circle on the little table in the shadowy hallway where they were now standing.

"We've been discovered in any case," he said finally, as if speaking to himself. "I remember Pino Giocondo and I'm sure he remembers me."

He folded his arms across his chest.

"He didn't see you," said Grazia. "And he certainly doesn't know who I am."

"He'll come back. He'll ask questions. He used to fix things for my father when I was a boy. They had a falling-out about something, I don't remember what."

"Well, that was all a long time ago, Toni. I'm sure he doesn't remember anything about it now."

Toni laughed out loud.

"Oh, I'm sure he does. That is what people do in little villages – they have nothing else to do apart from nurse old grievances. They do that very well indeed."

"You're talking nonsense. That old man wouldn't even recognise you, I'm sure. You haven't been back here for years."

"You don't understand how things work down here, Grazia."

Toni suddenly sniggered

"What could a *milanese* ever understand in any case?"

He pronounced the word with such disgust that Grazia blushed angrily.

"Apart from the fact that I'm actually from Monza, I don't know what it is that you ignorant southerners have against the *milanesi*?"

"*Ignoranti*! How dare you say that! The north is successful on the backs of southerners!"

"Perhaps, after all, where else could the southerners find work, certainly not in the south, where there's none to be had unless you have the right connections!"

Grazia's cutting remark silenced Toni who was only able to glare at her and shake his head vehemently. He looked as if he was about to hit her. Emily glanced anxiously at Grazia, who was busy staring Toni down and urging him to act.

"Why don't you go back to the north then?" he said lamely. "Go back to the crowds! Lead the way. Go back to your mighty city!"

He kicked the door open and went outside. He wanted to slam the door shut behind him, but its rusty hinges were not very obliging and this only added to his bad temper. Some plaster had fallen off the wall and Grazia bent down to pick up the pieces. She turned to look at Emily.

"One day I will leave Toni, make no mistake about that!"

44

Emily stared at the dent he had left in the rickety old door.

"Did I ever tell you he was about to separate from his wife before she went and got ill. She had money of her own, you know, so he decided to hang on and get his hands on it. He pulled that one off all right!"

Emily was just wondering what had happened to the money Toni's wife had left him when the door suddenly banged open and Toni ran in, out of breath, dry withered leaves sticking to his shirt.

"They're all looking at me!" he exclaimed, pointing a shaky finger in the direction of the wood and its hooded shadows. "Yes, yes, all of them hidden in the trees over there!"

He cursed his bad luck under his breath and crouched behind the door. Grazia seemed to melt again at the sight of him and spoke to him now in a soft cajoling voice.

"Who are these wicked people who want to hurt my little boy?"

Toni did not answer. He was too busy looking out of the window as if he could still see a crowd of faces staring after him. Grazia looked at Emily and shrugged her shoulders.

"I have to give in to him when he's like this," she whispered in English.

Toni had picked up the shotgun again and was muttering under his breath. He stood up, peered out of the window one last time and went into the kitchen where he poured himself a large glass of red wine.

"That's quite a lot of wine on an empty stomach," said Grazia, who had followed him into the kitchen.

"*Sempre lamentele*, Grazia," he said, shaking his head.

He sat down on a wicker chair and began cleaning his shotgun, to Grazia's evident annoyance. Then he counted the cartridges in his pocket and laid them out on the table in orderly clusters. Having drained the last dregs of wine in the bottle, he pushed the glass to one side to continue polishing the gun. Grazia knotted her hands together, looking from him to Emily and back again. She did not even feel like making fun of him now.

CHAPTER 6

THE IRISHMAN

Ricky Brown was standing at a street corner, close to where a group of men, sitting outside a small bar on the shady side of the street, were playing cards and downing glasses of grappa, one after the other. The bar owner had switched on the television set and its large screen drew some of the men away from their game of *scopa*. Ricky glanced at the programme through the open door and was surprised when he saw rugby players running up a muddy pitch and dodging each other bullishly to get at the ball. A game of Italian rugby. Ricky raised his eyebrows. Not football after all. And there were plenty of spectators. Even the old men had suddenly lost interest in wondering what this pale-skinned foreigner was doing in their tiny little town.

Ricky glanced curiously around him. Black-framed funeral proclamations lined one side of the wall. He read the names and tried half-heartedly to make sense of the rest. Next to that wall, there was a dilapidated old building of a mellow honey colour that had evidently seen better days, by the looks of the intricately-sculpted coat of arms that graced the arched doorway. He could not help but be impressed by the defiant pomposity of the elaborate wrought-iron balconies that jutted out at unlikely angles over the narrow street. A tall man like himself would walk by and crack his head open against them if he was not careful. The effect was then spoiled by someone having written a lurid anti-government message on a wall underneath one of the balconies.

Such slogans and protest banners were nothing new to Ricky Brown nor was his overturning of cars on the Falls Road the most aggressive act he had ever been involved in by any means. Ricky had spent more than one night in prison. He remembered taking an overzealous part in a political demonstration during which several windows had been broken. After that particular episode in which he had been caught out, his father, the postmaster of a small country town near Belfast, had not spoken to him for more than three months in a row. When he came to think of it, Ricky had not heard from his father for a good long while. Mr. Brown did not approve of his son's apparently senseless traipsing around Europe. "The boy's always had too many irons in the fire. We should have seen it coming," his father had declared. "Flighty, too many interests – look at Neil there! Why can't he follow his brother's example?" He would have liked to see Ricky settled down like his elder brother Neil, who worked as a trainee accountant in Belfast, in spite of his being the very same person who had got through his school exams with such difficulty. Ricky had been the bright one who hardly needed to open a book to pass his exams with flying colours, the one who won all the prizes at school and had been offered any number of university places that he had turned down, the apple of his mother's eye before her untimely death. Then he had got involved with a rock band that went touring around Europe one summer, ending up working briefly in Rome before he met and became besotted by Chiara Cellamare.

Suddenly she appeared at Ricky's side, carrying a plastic bag full of shopping. She looked distraught.

"Let's go home," she said. "I don't like these people here!"

"What do you mean?"

48

Chiara said nothing and Ricky drove fast through the labyrinthine streets, past the peeling election posters and groups of old men at street corners staring after them in astonishment

They went into the kitchen where Grazia was attempting to fix the handle of one of the cupboards. She held a rusty screwdriver in one hand and what looked like a hammer in the other. Chiara's father, meanwhile, sat perched on a stool, studying a tattered catalogue of old coins. A faded postcard from Venice that marked the place he was reading fluttered to the floor just as they walked past.

"Well, well, and where have you two been?" scolded Grazia. "You really might think of giving me a hand sometimes!"

Toni Cellamare suddenly amazed them all by slapping his thigh loudly and exclaiming as he held the catalogue aloft like a trophy.

"I've got them! I've got them upstairs in a box!" He gulped down a glass of wine and craned his neck to gauge the reaction of Grazia who had put the screwdriver away and was now stirring what looked like a stew, an impassive expression on her face.

"*San Dionigi*i!" exclaimed Toni, who had been born on this saint's day and consequently felt obliged to use his name at regular intervals. "Don't you care about it, Grazia? Doesn't it make you excited?"

Grazia took a pinch of salt and added it to the pan without changing her expression of complete indifference. "You're being ridiculous, Toni! Old coins aren't going to save you. Will you take them with you to your next hideout?"

Toni looked as if he was about to hit her and Ricky stepped forward instinctively, planting his large lanky frame between them.

"Toni, Toni, don't worry, we don't need to go anywhere else," he said in his hesitant Italian, glancing across at Chiara for reassurance.

Toni stared bleakly at the table, his fingers drawing a line along a crack in the wood. His other hand was a tight fist with white knuckles. When he opened the hand, revealing the marks left by his fingernails, he began slowly to crack one finger after the other.

"I'm fed up with you!" exclaimed Grazia.

Toni picked up the illustrated catalogue from the table and threw it in her direction, just missing her.

"I'll do something dreadful one day, just you wait and see if I don't!" He added a few colourful Italian expletives to round off his argument. "I know what this is all about! You *milanesi* think you're a race apart, don't you?"

Toni's face had taken on an odd hue, his dark eyes boring into Grazia's. Ricky and Chiara were looking anxiously at the angry couple. Grazia had changed colour too and she simply continued staring at Toni.

"I'm not having any of this! You're not going to start threatening me, do you hear!"

Toni stood staring at her, as if transfixed, and then he made a face. Chiara eagerly seized her chance to distract her father but it was no use. He pushed her hand aside and called after Grazia, who had, in the meantime, walked out of the kitchen.

"They're on my trail and you don't care, do you!" He looked stricken, a shell of a man standing there in his cotton vest, his flabby white arms hanging limply by his side.

He put out an imploring hand to Grazia; she ignored him and he followed her into the hallway, continuing to hector her with his entreaties.

Ricky sat down heavily on one of the rickety chairs and filled a glass full to the brim with ruby red wine. He raised his glass to Chiara who glared at him.

"It was a mistake to come here," she said glumly. "I didn't realise just what my father was like. He's losing his mind! I think we should go back to Rome as fast as possible!"

"Yeah, go back to Rome without a penny in our pockets!"

"You're forgetting what my mother left me."

Chiara threw her glossy black hair over her shoulders and began telling him for the hundredth time about her mother, managing to look simultaneously grief-stricken and over-sentimental. Ricky was not fooled; he knew fine well what she really felt about her mother. She had once described her in such coarse language that Ricky had had to beg her to stop, filled with compunction towards a woman who had died from the same kind of cancer that had killed his own mother.

"We could go away from here tomorrow. I'd only have to find a bank."

"How can we just leave them? Toni's going to end up killing Grazia. Why doesn't your saintly brother do something?"

"Francesco? Why should he do anything? He's too busy acting the missionary to bother about us, just like my mother was always too busy with her charitable works to think about her own family. We used to be the laughing-stock of the school, the only ones without proper pinafores, without pencil cases, without books, because our mother never had the time to think about such things!"

Ricky hated the way she would rave on about her unhappy childhood with a mother who had neglected her to dedicate her time to good works and a father who had dedicated his time in equal measure to other forms of amusement.

Emily was hovering about just outside the open kitchen door. When Chiara noticed her, she let out a heartfelt sigh and made eyes at Ricky. She could not in fact understand Emily's presence in the house. To Ricky in private, she had a nickname for the English woman, "*la candela*"; she considered her a lonely individual who had long outstayed her welcome. Ricky stood up and greeted Emily who smiled hesitantly at them both. She had no time to say anything however as there was suddenly a noise like someone tumbling down the stairs. Chiara put down the cup she had been drinking from and rushed out of the room in the direction of the sound, followed by Ricky and Emily. They stood at the foot of the staircase, staring in disbelief at Grazia who was in the process of violently dragging an enormous suitcase down the stairs. Sweat dotted her forehead but she still managed to find the strength to call Toni names. She stopped short at the sight of Chiara.

"Yes, my dear, and just think that I almost married your father. I would have become your stepmother – that would have been quite a joke, wouldn't it!"

Toni lay almost prone on the landing, grasping at Grazia's ankles and generally hindering her process down the stairs.

"We'll find the hidden money, I promise you. Grazia, just give me a little more time!"

"*Tu sei impazzito!*"

Grazia pushed him curtly aside and faced the others.

"No, don't look at me like that! You don't know the half of his boorish behaviour. Certainly, Chiara, you'll be feeling relieved I have no intention of taking your saintly mother's place!"

"Well, you're quite right there! Actually I'm glad you're leaving us!" announced Chiara summarily, to everybody's astonishment. "You treat my father like he was some kind of criminal! I've had enough of you and I'm sure my father has too!"

"No, no, Grazia, don't listen to her," said Toni with vehemence in his voice. "It's all nonsense what she's saying!"

He had managed to get past her on the stairs and was now standing woodenly in front of her, blocking her passage. They were all silent now, so silent that the sound of a pin dropping would have made them turn their heads in its direction. Grazia held her handbag poised above Toni's head as if she were wielding a cudgel. Ricky and Emily glanced at each other out of the corner of their eyes. He scratched his head and finally managed to muster up enough courage to break the spell of silence and address everyone in stentorian tones.

"Why do you all have to carry on like martinets? Let's just calm down, everybody."

Toni turned around slowly, looking at Ricky as if seeing him for the first time.

"Well, Ricky Brown, I don't think any of us could care less about what you think! You're a complete jerk, do you hear!"

Toni Cellamare, who was a man of smallish stature, apparently grew so much in size as he spoke so belligerently that he gave the impression of being almost the same height as Ricky. Chiara glanced anxiously at her boyfriend to gauge his reaction.

"Don't think I don't know all about you and your anarchist friends!"

Ricky looked at Toni with a cantankerous expression stamped on his features.

"Are you out of your mind, *papà*?" exclaimed Chiara hotly on behalf of her oddly silent boyfriend.

"Oh, I know all about Ricky Brown, the way you act so sanctimoniously while you surround yourself with terrorists. Don't think I don't know all about your activities! You think you can pull my daughter down with you – well, I'm not having it any more, do you hear!"

Toni began to laugh, a little hysterically, and Grazia stared at him in astonishment, perhaps marvelling also at his sudden fluent grasp of the English language. She even tried to utter a few healing words in Toni's direction but it was now Chiara's turn to speak.

"What are you going to do about it, anyway? We congratulate you on your detective skills. You're a regular

Sherlock Holmes, *papà*. Well, you might be interested to know that I'm in on this too before Ricky ever was! In fact, I'd be the one risking prison."

"What group do you belong to?" asked Toni, looking incredulous.

"Oh, what does it matter? Call us anarchists if you like." She was speaking quietly, but, suddenly, she looked him full in the face and began insulting him, hurling abuse at him in a high-pitched tone of voice.

"How dare you insult Ricky! *Canaglia*!"

She continued in the same vein, making such a din that Emily, at the foot of the stairs, was tempted to run from the house just to get away from the noise. She felt a hand on her shoulder and turned around to see Ricky staring at her with his cool grey eyes.

"Hey, Emmy, let's get out of here. I've had enough arguments for one day."

They slipped out of the house without anyone saying anything; they could still hear raised voices. Emily blinked in the sunlight. Ricky sat down on a stone bench and began to roll himself a cigarette. He offered her one but she shook her head and remained standing.

"I'm fed up with the lot of them!" he said. "They're all shouting now. Can you hear them?" He nodded in the direction of the open window. "I can't stand all their arguing! That's why Chiara calls me a coward."

Emily took a long sidelong glance at him. He did not look like a coward to her. In fact, if only he had been wearing a doublet and hose and a cigarette had not been burning between his fingers, he would have looked as if he might just that moment have stepped out of a Shakespearian tragedy.

"Have you fulfilled your dreams out here in Italy?" he suddenly asked her.

Emily shook her head sadly. "I don't go in for dreams nowadays. I had them dashed once too often when I was younger."

"Really," he said, looking at her with renewed interest. "I'm sure they would make for interesting telling. Let's get out of here, first of all."

CHAPTER 7

THE HUNTER

They were sitting at a table outside a small bar beside the nearest petrol station. Emily had got on the Vespa somewhat reluctantly, imagining what Chiara might have to say on their return to the farmhouse. She smoothed her dress down and turned around to admire the countryside that stretched out into the distance, appreciatively sniffing the sweet fragrance of a nearby fig tree laden with fruit. Ricky's appealing grey eyes were beginning to have a curious effect on her and she tried her best to remind herself that he was at least fifteen years younger than her. Then there was his potentially homicidal girlfriend to reckon with, undoubtedly more than ready to stab Emily to death if she even thought of getting up to anything with him.

"Don't you miss city life at all?" he asked her, putting down his cup of cappuccino. She had given up drinking cappuccinos in the afternoons a long time ago, fed up with the arch little smiles of superiority that the Italian barmen used to give her. It was not the kind of thing that Ricky would ever notice. Emily had ordered a Campari, the taste of it always rather disappointing but the bright red colour entrancing her every time.

"No, I can't say I miss it," she said. "The countryside's so pretty hereabouts. Anyway, I can't stay holed up here forever, I know that much."

"And what are you going to do next?"

"Oh, I'm not sure. I'm not even close to deciding. That's always been my problem, you know!"

"Well, something's bound to happen up at the farmhouse. I'm not sure I want to hang around to watch!"

"What do you mean?"

"The way they tried to kill Chiara's father – what if they try again?"

"How would they find out where he is?"

"Oh, that's where I think you're all wrong. The deserted family home is the most obvious place in the world. Even if it wasn't, they could easily have followed Chiara and me. We could have led them to him!"

"Don't you think you should tell Toni all this?"

"Oh no, I want to have as little to do with him as possible. He's a funny guy and no mistake. He'll be the one who ends up shooting the lot of us! What are we all doing here, that's what I'd like to know. You and me shouldn't be involved in any of this. We're the ones who have a pressing need to get away! Believe you me, things are about to take a serious turn for the worse…"

Twisting a paper napkin around her finger, Emily was looking quite taken aback at what he had just said and began to stare fixedly at the white plastic table as if her life depended upon it.

The little bar was getting crowded. The bus from Foggia had just stopped and a chattering group of oversized middle-aged women piled in, pushing and shoving each other loudly and glancing curiously at Ricky and Emily as they passed.

Somewhere in the distance, a silvery train flashed past. Emily was wondering where it was going to; the next minute, she was blurting out the story of her life to Ricky.

"Heaven knows what I'm doing here in Italy again," she said finally. "Can you tell me what I'm looking for?"

"Why do you imagine you'll find whatever you're looking for here?"

Ricky was speaking in his usual laconic tone of voice, but there was something in the way that his grey eyes bored into her that made her feel uncomfortable.

"I don't think you're going to find a solution to your problems here," he continued. "You've just created distance between yourself and your problems."

Emily stared at the spindly table leg in front of her and wondered if he was right.

"You should get in touch with your sister again. So what does it matter if she's gone and married someone you don't like? Go back to Britain. After all, no family can possibly be more peculiar than *la famiglia Cellamare*!"

Emily shrugged her shoulders and Ricky continued in the same vein.

"What I can't understand is the way your Grazia has stuck by that old nutter. She should be in Milan, running her own business – some kind of Prada success story. She's that kind of woman. She shouldn't be pandering to that old waster!"

"Francesco should talk to both of them."

"The handsome priest, you mean." Ricky smirked. "I don't see how he can be of much use – he's still pining away for his dead mother. Chiara's told me her brother is the kind of person who is unable to cope with modern society and I certainly can't be bothered with anyone connected to the Catholic Church."

Emily looked pensive and more subdued than ever – her only reaction now was to shake her head and press her lips more tightly together. Sitting here with Ricky and talking so intimately about the Cellamare family, she half-expected Chiara to barge in on them at any moment. Ricky, meanwhile, had ordered a bottle of grappa and was filling her glass to the brim, splashing it liberally on the paper tablecloth. It made Emily feel a little dizzy.

"What we need to do is to get away from here. I've been trying to persuade Chiara it would be the right thing to do, but she listens to that silly old fool. He'll be the death of all of us one day. He's losing his head! Have you seen him going through his collection of old weapons up in the attic? Well, I have, and it was quite an experience, I can assure you. He lifted up a… I can't even remember the name of the thing now… A kind of rifle, anyway, and he levelled it at me and threatened to shoot me. I think he saw his chance if you get what I mean."

Ricky spoke softly, but the more softly he spoke, the more the regular customers standing at the bar seemed to be staring at him.

"He tried to provoke me, shouting names at me, standing there with that old gun pointing at me."

"Didn't you tell Chiara?"

"Of course I told her. She just said his old guns were never loaded. It's the hunting rifle he keeps downstairs we should be worried about, she said! You know the one, the one Grazia would like to hide in her kitchen cupboards – as if that wouldn't be the first place he'd look!"

Ricky sighed heavily and looked quickly at Emily to gauge her reaction. She was sitting there as quiet as a mouse in her crumpled dress, perhaps unperturbed, or, perhaps, only half-listening. He was not at all sure what to make of her, particularly when she suddenly smiled archly and made an announcement.

"Don Francesco's coming back soon. He'll be able to put matters right between everybody, I'm sure."

Ricky smiled thinly. He did not like priests. Was Emily secretly in love with Francesco Cellamare? Why else would she be so enthusiastic about his imminent arrival? Out of the corner of his eye, he studied her: straight nose, light blue eyes and the thin lined mouth that went and spoiled everything.

"Well," he said at last. "I suppose Francesco doesn't get into a state the way the rest of them do. He hardly seems Italian at all, apart from the way he looks, I mean. He's very good-looking, isn't he?"

"Oh, I've hardly noticed – what with those long black robes he always wears. They make him sexless somehow."

Ricky didn't believe her, but said nothing. He poured himself out another glass of grappa. It was very good and he glanced at the label: Trentino, of course, and he started thinking of the mountains. With any luck, he could go skiing at Christmas if he got some cash together. While he was musing like this, he caught snatches of conversation from the group of old men standing at the bar under the ceiling fan and realised that he and Emily were being talked about and not in the most flattering of terms. He swivelled around to get a better look. Emily turned too and immediately noticed that Pino Giocondo, the old man with the shotgun, was one of them.

A large dog wandered over to their table and just stood there, looking up at Emily. Ricky glanced warily at it; he was not overly fond of dogs, particularly large ones.

"Perhaps we should be heading back now," he said.

Emily smiled at his evident discomfort, even if she deliberately kept her hands on the table and pretended to ignore the dog. Pino Giocondo, the dog's owner, approached them and rewarded them with what he must have imagined was a winning smile, albeit somewhat toothless.

"It must be hot sitting outside today," he said. He spoke imperfect English but with the genuine American twang of a one-time emigrant. They were both surprised to hear him speak English. Emily took a better look at him, shading her eyes against the sun.

"Oh, I was born in the States," he said brightly. "A very long time ago of course."

He sat down without being asked and picked up the bottle of grappa, glancing at it with an expert eye.

"You won't mind me drinking with you," he said, throwing a meaningful look in Emily's direction. "After all, it's not often I have the opportunity to talk to a beautiful English lady."

Emily broke into an embarrassed, high-pitched laugh and Pino's dog, sitting at his master's feet, whimpered at the strange sound.

"Look, *signorina*, your glass is cracked. Maria, bring another glass for our English friend and one for me too. You don't mind if I join you both?"

He did not expect an answer and leaned down to pet his dog that immediately lay prostrate waiting to be tickled. Maria, the large unlovely bartender, trudged over to the table, bearing the glasses in one hand and dragging a broom along the floor in the other.

Pino carefully poured out generous measures of grappa for the three of them and sipped his slowly with the air of a connoisseur.

"I've known Antonio Cellamare a long time now," he said, choosing his words deliberately and lighting the cigarette that Ricky offered him. "Oh yes, I used to be friendly with Enrico, that's Antonio's big brother. I don't suppose he's ever mentioned his big brother to either of you. They never did get on. They say poor Enrico died in mysterious circumstances. Disappeared anyway... never found as much as a trace of him ever again. They even suspected Antonio for a bit... Maybe he was jealous of him and the inheritance..."

Pino Giocondo's eyes had become wild and lunatic-looking as he told this tale, to Ricky and Emily's utter bemusement.

"I don't know what you're all up to in that old house, but I say prayers for you!"

He fell silent, his wild gaze finally settling on the distant hills. Then he wrinkled his long nose and downed the remainder of the grappa all at once.

"Well, I hope I haven't bored you. I thought you should be warned, that's all."

Emily shuffled her feet under the table, suddenly overcome by the desire to get away. Ricky, on the other hand, seemed to have no intention whatsoever of moving anywhere. He continued staring at Pino.

"Why don't you come by some time?" he said. "After all… if you're such an old friend of the family."

Pino smiled affably at Ricky, taking a sudden liking to this young foreigner.

"And tell me, where exactly do you come from with that accent? Not from Brooklyn anyway?"

"I'm from Ireland."

"Really! Well, there were plenty of Irishmen in New York – good people, like the Italians. I used to go to an Irish pub for the westerns. Oh, I love westerns, John Ford movies, all that kind of thing. Do you like them?"

Ricky nodded and the old man now turned around to take a better look at Emily, leering unpleasantly and giving her a friendly pat on her bare back with callused hands that made her stiffen instinctively.

"Well, why don't you both come along to my house," he said. "It's not often I get the chance to speak English. Certainly, the path up to it is a bit muddy." He looked hesitantly at Emily's sandals. "You'll have to forgive the chairs in my kitchen too. It's an old, old house, should have been knocked down a long time ago!"

He waved in the direction of the wooden trellis that leant against the wall. The two old men at the bar turned around to stare at him; one of them shouted out in dialect in a voice of genuine concern.

"*Pino mio*, what's the matter with you? You've turned a strange colour!"

He was indeed looking very flushed and his eyes roved around in a peculiar way. Visibly, he shook himself.

"Come on then!" he said at last.

Ricky smiled and nodded at Emily, who continued to sit stiffly on the edge of the plastic seat. The old man stood up and shook out his threadbare jacket. Smiling faintly, he threw the cigarette butt on to the ground and pointed a menacing finger at the splendid cerulean sky.

"It's been too dry for too long! We need water for the fields. Everything's drying up." He spoke in a disgusted tone of voice. "Oh, I realise it's fine weather for tourists like the pair of you. That's what you are, isn't it – tourists, I mean?"

The dog was jumping around him now, gazing up at him with beseeching eyes.

"You like to visit places in your smart city clothes," he said, ignoring the overexcited dog at his heels. "I could tell you plenty more interesting stories, ones you'd never find in any of your guidebooks. I could tell you plenty about the Cellamare family too, how they used to act like tax collectors round here, getting rent paid to them. Oh, they used to own a lot of land, you know, and they made us pay through our teeth for the use of it!"

Emily and Ricky, pushing the Vespa along a sloping path hemmed in by ravines, followed the old man through an olive grove, Ricky whispering in Emily's ear comments like this.

"I do believe this is going to be extremely interesting – we now have an incomparable guide to the intimate secrets of the

Cellamare family, all those things that dear old Toni has never told anybody…"

The dog began barking as they rounded a corner and saw an old tumbledown house with a ramshackle roof in the middle of a clearing.

"This is where I live," said Pino. "It's not up to much, I know, and to think we came back from America with a fortune in our pockets. My poor mother had to end her days living in poverty. All thanks to the Cellamare family – oh, but Toni will reap his reward one day too, you'll see. He's got so cocky, he would pass me by in the street as if I were a stranger!"

An ancient cart stood outside the simple square house. Three more dogs were making a tremendous din from behind a mesh contraption that acted as a door.

"Well, my friends, meet the family," said Pino, letting the dogs out. They leapt up at him, practically knocking him over. "Now Lilli here is quite intelligent, really. She's the female. Pucci is quite another matter – the stupidest dog I've ever had in my life. He'll disappear and forget his way home and I have to go out looking for him!"

Pino led them through a long, dark, low-ceilinged corridor, past cluttered piles of fishing rods, useless reels and a rusty shotgun, into a kitchen that was similarly overloaded with sundry objects and which immediately gave an impression of untidy disarray. It was, however, pleasantly cool and there was a nice view of the trees out of the large window. The house was very quiet – not a sound from the road reached them. Ricky and Emily sat down at the long trestle table, where a pile of dusty books was leaning precariously to one side, propped up against an enormous jar of salted capers. Emily noticed that the book on top of the pile was by Gabriele D'Annunzio; the idea of Pino reading his poetry amazed her. Pino noticed her look of surprise but added no revealing comment about his choice of literature.

"What do you think of my little house then?" he asked. "It's not up to very much, I know. The olive trees no longer give fruit but I can grow vegetables out the back here – you should see my aubergines." He paused and went over to a cupboard. "Can I offer you something to eat now?"

Ricky, who was very hungry, nodded his head. Pino placed a bottle of what must have been homemade wine on the table and took down some glasses from the cupboard.

"I could tell you plenty about those Cellamare. They're a bad lot – always have been, oh, apart from the current generation perhaps. No, I'll tell you about Toni Cellamare's father – a hard man if ever there was one – a stubborn man who always had to have his own way, even if it meant getting his hands dirty! He was the one who evicted us. *Che bastardo!*"

Suddenly he got up and began storming around the kitchen. Ricky was thoroughly enjoying the situation and watched Pino in fascination as he marched up and down the kitchen, brandishing his rough peasant hands in the air, in an apparent imitation of Mussolini. A distant roll of thunder and a flash of lightning provided a suitably theatrical backdrop to Pino's long tirade.

"He threw the lot of you out, but that's terrible!" declared Ricky, throwing Emily a mocking smile.

Pino was becoming more and more agitated, while Emily sat as quiet as a mouse, inwardly terror-stricken, on her uncomfortably hard chair.

"Apart from evicting the lot of you, did he do anything else?" insisted Ricky. The gleam of amusement in Ricky's eyes was completely lost on Pino.

"Oh yes, he certainly did, but... oh, something too terrible to mention. I couldn't even talk about that, no, no! This isn't the moment to talk about that."

Pino's evasive speech annoyed Ricky, whose curiosity had been whetted.

"Why don't you tell us?" he said abruptly. "We won't tell anyone."

Pino looked at the two of them with raised eyebrows and continued his tale.

"It all happened just before the last war, I suppose, not long after us getting off that ship from America, and after my father died. My father was an able man out there in New York, but he was thin and delicate. My mother now, she was a woman to be reckoned with – black hair, big, a little ungainly perhaps and she did love to cover herself in trinkets!"

Pino hesitated and looked at them to see what their reaction might be. Ricky nodded at him in encouragement, so Pino carried on telling them about this mother of his, who, by the sound of things, had brought trouble on herself by her immodest behaviour in a small town in small-minded southern Italy. Pino droned on interminably, the only other sound in the kitchen being the incessant creaking of the hinges of the back door that had not been shut properly.

Emily was bored; she gazed at the kitchen ceiling where the plaster was peeling off and there were large damp patches in the corners. Occasionally, Ricky would pose a cleverly phrased question to bring the conversation back to the, by all accounts, dissolute Cellamare family. Pino set another bottle of wine on the table with a thud.

"There's only one way of describing them – *banda di diavoli*! We had to leave my father's house and come here to live!" He thudded the table with his clenched fist. "And now the son calls himself *dottore* and acts as if he had been born in Rome, but I know all about him too, oh yes, and that arrogant father of his, who thought he could just kick out the tenant farmers whenever he felt like it! But he couldn't have imagined the trouble he was sowing for himself!"

Wind suddenly began to rattle the windowpanes and the black scarecrow that Pino had placed amongst his vegetables was now waving at them in a grotesque, surreal way.

Pino drank another glass of wine and muttered darkly under his breath about the coming Day of Judgement. It all sounded excessively dramatic to Emily, sitting on her wobbly chair and trying in vain to catch Ricky's eye so that they could make a move and go away.

Pino put a hand through his white hair, then he opened a tin of tobacco and rolled a cigarette for himself with an air of zealous concentration. Bowing courteously, he offered the first one to Emily; she shook her head and he gave it to Ricky.

"Why didn't you ever report their goings-on to the *carabinieri*?" asked Ricky, inhaling deeply.

Pino's mouth curled up in a sneer.

"One of his uncles was the *maresciallo*, another was *sindaco* – this one was more corrupt than most so he ended up getting himself shot at the end of the war."

"And when did this mayor get himself shot exactly?"

"Oh, you don't believe me, is that it? I'll call someone to confirm my story…"

"No, no, why shouldn't I believe you," said Ricky quickly. The last thing he wanted was to quarrel with Pino Giocondo.

"Perhaps you're wondering why I want to stir things up. I should mind my own business, eh? I wanted to warn you, that's all – he's spiteful and mean like his father before him and he'll get you all into trouble! He's just playing with you all at the moment maybe but he's a destructive man, you mark my words!"

"Oh, we won't be here for much longer, I can assure you. We'll be going back to Rome soon," said Ricky, throwing Emily a meaningful glance.

Pino calmed down a little when he heard this. He got up from his chair to let the barking dogs out.

"When are we going to Rome exactly?" asked Emily in Ricky's ear, her face suddenly brightening up. "What, just the two of us?"

She looked almost pretty and he nodded his head slowly, mulling over what he had just said. Chiara thought theirs was a love that would last forever.

"It would be best for the pair of you if you left as soon as possible," said Pino, coming back and banging his fist again on the table. "Toni Cellamare has made too many mistakes and there's no one here who can save him now!"

"Why don't you go and speak to him yourself?" asked Ricky in a quiet voice.

Pino threw him a triumphant look.

"I think you're right, my boy!" he suddenly exclaimed. "I could even go over there and punch him on the nose!"

Emily was astonished. What was Ricky up to? Why was he inciting Pino to go and confront Toni Cellamare?

Pino stood up and went over to the window, where he gazed outside for a long time, a grim expression on his face. When he finally roused himself from his reverie and turned around to look at them again, his eyes were red and bulging.

"I could go and slip into his house right now!" His eyes began to sparkle at the thought.

He went out of the room again and came back with a large sheaf of papers in his hands. He thudded them down on the table in front of Ricky, knocking over a basket of walnuts in the process. He threw Ricky a long, meaningful look and paid no heed to the walnuts scattered over the floor.

"Have a look at these papers, my boy!" he said in his most commanding voice. "They prove that the house and land around it really belong to my family!"

Pino stood up, making his back as straight as possible, his arms outstretched in the manner of a priest reciting his Sunday sermon.

"I thought you said the Cellamare had plenty of money of their own in any case," said Ricky.

"Oh, money – what's money compared to the best land in the district! And my grandfather had the best land in the whole area – even the wood used to belong to him!"

"And you're quite sure that Toni knows all about the house not being his. I mean, why would he come back here at all, after all these years, if he wasn't sure it was his house?"

Pino evidently did not feel the need to explain matters any further. He just nodded in the direction of the papers.

"Those documents don't leave anything out," he said abruptly, opening the back door and following one of the dogs outside.

"Ricky, why do you keep on encouraging that old man? It's as if you were daring him to have a go at Toni. I don't understand you."

"Oh, you'd understand fast enough if you had ever thought of Toni Cellamare as one of your closest relations. I wanted to get married, you know, before... well, the message arrived that I just wasn't welcome...No, no, the bastard didn't leave anything out!" Ricky clenched and unclenched his fists in his lap. "He began writing me a kind of hate mail, very personal stuff, all in Italian of course, so I had to read them with my dictionary!" He gazed blankly at a damp patch above the cobweb-festooned window.

"You're maybe wondering why I mention all this. I can see what you're like, Emily, the kind of person who would let everybody off the hook! No, no, don't look at me like that either, like some kind of consumptive heroine, like Elizabeth Barret Browning!"

"She wasn't consumptive!" said Emily tartly.

Ricky guffawed loudly at this.

"Oh, you know perfectly well what I mean – you're the kind who always sticks up for the losers! You might even stick up for me one day!'"

Pino had come back into the kitchen, this time burdened by another heavy basket of walnuts.

Emily was desperate to leave. She wanted Ricky all to herself but he ignored her entirely and turned his attention back to Pino.

"I think Toni Cellamare should pay a penalty for all the suffering he's caused you and your family," he said.

When Pino turned his face towards him, Emily was taken aback at the sight of such a brutal expression of loathing.

"You're right, *giovanotto*, you're absolutely right!"

In spite of Emily trying to make herself look as inconspicuous as possible, Pino walked over to her and looked her straight in the eye, making her redden. He continued standing close to her, his dark brigand's face looming fierce and threatening.

"Are you intimate then with Toni, *signorina*?" he asked her at last. "He always was a charmer with the ladies."

Emily shook her head vigorously and he turned his gloomy attention elsewhere, out of the window this time, at the hills in the distance, where Toni's house had to be, and took a sudden intake of breath.

"You'd better get going, the pair of you. It's getting late. Here's a bag of the best walnuts you'll ever taste!"

Pino led them out along the dark dingy corridor, where they glimpsed another labyrinthine corridor in the grey gloom as well as a steep staircase that disappeared under a low sloping roof. There were the remains of what could once have been a stream at the bottom of the garden where Ricky had parked the Vespa. They went past the barking dogs with not a little trepidation. Ricky promised Pino that he would come back to visit him soon. Pino looked glum, continuing to stare into the distance and apparently oblivious to what the young man was saying to him. Ricky drove carefully up the rocky verge and took the first sharp bend they came to, just as Pino had told him. The winding road through the olive grove was little more than a path, dotted with boulders that had tumbled down the slope and had never been cleared away. Emily felt anxious and clung all the more tightly to Ricky. When they passed a white-haired old man, another one carrying a shotgun carelessly slung over one shoulder, she got such a fright she almost fell off the moped. Ricky did not even seem to notice; he was too busy thinking about what he was going to say to Chiara.

***

Toni Cellamare was standing outside in what was left of the sunshine. At the sound of the Vespa's engine, he disappeared inside once again, leaving Ricky laughing.

"Here we go again, still acting the little fascist pig I see, creeping about the place with his shotgun over his shoulder!" He sounded irritated. "What a bore it all is!"

"Oh, why did I ever come here, Ricky?" asked Emily suddenly.

"I've no idea. You should be asking yourself that question, not me."

"I suppose I just wanted to get away."

She sounded so thoroughly depressed that Ricky resisted answering her with sarcasm. He only shrugged his shoulders.

The house was in semi-darkness after the summer brightness and Ricky almost stumbled over the doormat. Fumbling for a light switch, Emily suddenly found herself confronting the steely determined expression of an executioner: Chiara. Then, just as suddenly, she looked past Emily and stared all aglow at Ricky who returned her gaze with a rueful, roguish smile, enough to make her run breathlessly into his open arms. It was all too much for Emily; she slipped past them up the dimly-lit stairs to her bedroom where she began packing her things together. She had no idea where she was going; all she knew was that she had to get away.

"Where the hell do you think you're going?" announced Grazia suddenly, shutting the door silently behind her. "No, no, you can't leave me alone here!"

The tone of her voice had become a pleading one, quite unlike the Grazia that Emily had used to know.

"Look, I just don't see the point of me staying on here…" Emily said lamely.

"You don't see the point! What about me then? I wasn't exactly trained as a nurse for the mentally ill!"

Grazia came over and stood very close to Emily. With a sinking heart, the English woman waited for her Italian friend to throw her arms around her neck. She may have been about to, but, whatever her intentions, they were interrupted by a long, terrifying screech. Grazia hurried over to the window.

"What was that?" asked Emily, her face as white as a ghost.

"Oh, that – just an owl. Yes, we now have an owl in one of the pine trees, two perhaps. Toni can't stand it – he says he's going to shoot them. Owls bring bad luck, he says. He'll be outside right now with his shotgun!"

Emily was speechless.

"He can't do that. He's cruel!" She was thinking much worse things about Toni Cellamare, but she kept them to herself. Grazia read her thoughts.

"I know, I know, he's an utter thug, completely mad into the bargain!"

Shots rang out and Grazia managed to wrench the stiff window wide open. She had tanned muscular arms and she leaned out of the window, her thick hair coming undone, and began shouting Toni's name into the twilight. Emily stayed where she was, motionless near the bed, watching Grazia gradually relax her grip on the windowsill. Above the bed, there was a picture of the Madonna; underneath it, amber-coloured rosary beads hung down the wall. Grazia went over to the picture, her hands clasped tightly together in an imploring gesture. Emily could hardly believe this was the same person who had once spoken of the Church with such loathing; now here she was kneeling beside the bed, overcome by a rush of piety.

"*Dio mio*, Toni says he is beginning to think I must have hired those assassins in Rome, can you believe it? He thinks I want to get rid of him! He thinks I've become greedy – I want to get my hands on his money!" Grazia looked disgusted at the very idea.

"Don't you ever feel worried about him doing something silly out here, something violent maybe?"

"Oh, he is incapable of action now, violent or otherwise," said Grazia derisively, walking over to the window once more and letting out an irritated sigh.

Emily wondered what she could say to comfort her. She looked helplessly around the sparsely-furnished bedroom; the whitewashed walls, peeling in places, were bare apart from the picture of the Madonna above the bed and some incongruous prints from Alessandro Manzoni's "*I Promessi Sposi*" lining one wall. The central one was bigger than the others and depicted a distinguished-looking gentleman being carried along in a sedan chair. Grazia looked at them too.

"A little corner of Milan in Puglia," she commented peevishly. "What the hell are we doing here, the pair of us?"

Emily bit her lip uncertainly.

"I've lost touch with all my old friends because of him, you know!" announced Grazia. "My brother can't stand Toni either. The last time I tried to speak to Giovanni, he put the phone down on me because he heard Toni's voice in the background."

Emily felt awkward and unsure of what to say. Grazia fell silent and got up to bolt the door. She lay down on the bed,

Emily sitting down beside her, a deep frown creasing her forehead. Grazia looked grief-stricken, an entirely different woman to the one who had barely put up with Emily's company not so long ago in Rome.

Grazia unbuttoned her dress and threw it onto a chair, knocking over a basket of potpourri that fell noiselessly to the floor. She curled herself up on the bed, wrapping the sheet around her. Somewhere in the distance, fireworks were going off in the sky. Emily stood looking at them from the windowsill, bleakly wondering how she had ever managed to get involved in such an emotional mess. Was there ever going to be any way out?

CHAPTER 8

IN THE WOODS

Emily was woken up by the sound of Grazia screaming and shouting at the top of her voice. She listened to the sound dying down until it was little more than a broken whimper of sorts. Toni had evidently entrenched himself inside his bedroom. She glanced at her watch. Just after six. With an irritated sigh, she got up, feeling cold and really rather loath to go and see what all the noise was about.

A row of brightly-coloured tin soldiers was perfectly aligned outside Toni's bedroom door; the slightly larger, crooked figure of a general had been kicked over by Grazia, who was now standing quietly against the wall, her eyes rimmed with dark tell-tale shadows. She was on the point of saying something when the pealing of distant bells suddenly broke into the quiet of Toni Cellamare's dingy lair.

"*Si, si, la festa del santo padrone*!" muttered Grazia under her breath, turning her face in the direction of the sound just in time to see Ricky coming up the stairs and crossing the landing.

"Well, it won't be the battle of Waterloo, that's for sure!" he said laconically, unbuttoning his denim jacket. Emily wondered where he had been at such an early hour. Ricky read her thoughts.

"I was just taking a walk when I happened to bump into Pino again – he had a gun slung over his shoulder. I wonder if he has a permit for it – not that it would really matter in this godforsaken corner of the earth!" Ricky smiled and bent down to Emily. "Oh, and by the way, Emmy, he told me he doesn't want to be kept waiting for our next little visit to him."

Grazia looked horrified.

"Pino Giocondo! I can't believe you've been to see him behind Toni's back!"

"And why shouldn't we see him? We can do what we like, can't we? What's it to you?" said Ricky.

Grazia looked aghast.

"Toni hates him!"

"Why should he hate this man from his own town? They've known each other for such a long time. But the funny thing is that Pino Giocondo hates Toni Cellamare too, in spite of or maybe because of their long acquaintance!"

"Is that what he told you?" asked Grazia.

"We were certainly able to deduce it," said Emily, trying to sound calm and collected.

"But I still can't understand why you went to his house, Emily?"

"I went with him," said Emily lamely, nodding in Ricky's direction.

He stood opposite the two women, staring at them a little defiantly. Emily had moved nearer to Grazia, on the defensive and seeming to side with her. Grazia was about to speak when Toni suddenly opened the bedroom door and began a long noisy tirade, directed entirely at Grazia, who was now looking wearier than ever. Ugly, untranslatable invectives poured out of his snarling mouth. Ricky grabbed hold of Emily's arm and pulled her with him down the stairs.

"Listen, we have to get out of here now! Let's go away, the two of us. What's the point of staying on here, for God's sake?"

Emily said nothing, only shaking her head sadly and looking down at the floor.

"Well, I have to get out of here, that's for sure."

"I can't just abandon Grazia, can I?"

"Look, doesn't she have family of her own who can be looking after her. Isn't that the Italian way of doing things?"

"I suppose it is…" she answered slowly, looking around at the drab furnishings as if she might find inspiration there.

She turned around to go back upstairs to Grazia. Ricky grabbed her elbow; Emily felt the strength in his large hand.

"What can you do here anyway?" he said. "They all take offence so easily! I'm fed up with it. I thought you were too."

"Fed up with Chiara too?" she asked, unwittingly managing to sound hopeful

Ricky fell momentarily silent.

"I'm fed up with Italy, that's all, or, at least, this refuse dump of a backwater. I'm fed up with being here."

He turned away from Emily. Chiara was still asleep upstairs. He had no idea what he was going to do about Chiara. He might even have gone to university if he had not gone and bumped into her. The very first time he had seen her, she had been wearing a flimsy top with silver sequins and he had fallen in love, as simple as that. Working together every evening in the bar in London, they would go back to his flat afterwards and make love all night. Heavenly, hedonistic days. When they had days off, they would go and buy up the local supermarket, take all the stuff home and remain closed inside the house until they ran out of food. That was when he started not to bother any more about planning for his future, the way his irritating father would have liked. How could the very idea of studying anything compare with Chiara's overt charms? A promising student, one of his teachers had got in touch with him personally to ask him why he had not gone to university like all his other brilliant pupils. Chiara had been taken aback by all this attention that she had called positively oppressive. That was when her own father had suddenly decided to turn up in London; he had been so affable to begin with, so charming and easy-going, remedying Chiara's various debts without batting an eyelid, so unlike Ricky's own rigidly puritanical tight-fisted father. Brown senior was obsessive about his spotless reputation; Ricky's brother had fallen neatly into line and was exactly his idea of a model son, Ricky anything but. It did take Ricky a little while to realise, but he eventually worked it out for himself, that his kind of father was a lot better than one like Toni Cellamare. They could not hide their feelings for each other for very long. They were going to set out for Italy, the three of them, when Ricky suddenly began to pick up some of the talk in Italian. It was all swearing and insults directed at him. Well, he was unable to keep his own mouth shut after that, of course, and the crude frankness of their shouting matches meant they didn't speak to each other for another six months. Toni had gone back to Italy on his own and had refused point-blank to give Chiara any more money. He had said they would just have to make ends meet.

"It's all rubbish, you're just making it all up! Why do you have to listen to that old man?"

"This house belongs to the Giocondo family – that's what he told me!"

Emily was only too relieved to hear that Ricky and Chiara were not in fact arguing about her. Chiara punctuated every sentence she uttered with an irritated sigh that made her body sway and her white skirt twirl around her slender brown legs, not to mention that way she had of throwing her long silky hair over her shoulders. She managed to exude both rude health and glamour and Emily could not help but admire her grace as she paced up and down. Ricky must have been of a similar opinion; he kept reaching out for her hands and trying to make up with her. It was all too much for Emily. She went outside.

Sparrows cavorting happily along the path flew off at the sound of her footsteps. A cool breeze blew through the pine trees and she felt her spirits lifted. She walked on through the verdant undergrowth that grew unchecked amongst the beech trees, wondering what she should do with herself. From where she was now standing, the house looked like such an insignificant little place. It seemed incredible that anyone would ever want to argue or fight over it. However, the soil around the house was the best in the area, Pino had assured them, a genuine paradise for vine-growers, with the best sunny slopes within a hundred kilometre radius; not too much sun either, and just the right amount of shade, to produce wine that could rival the best Chianti in Italy.

Emily was brought up short by the sight of litter strewn across the path. She meandered on, puzzling over who might have dropped empty cans of beer in this remote place. She had thought that nobody came to the wood apart from them and Pino of course. There was a rickety old hand-cart at the side of the overgrown path and Emily turned around, wondering whether Pino was about somewhere among the hooded shadows. All of a sudden, a man with a sallow face in singular contrast to his black beard and dishevelled hair appeared from behind the cart. He said *buongiorno* to Emily, who had jumped at his sudden appearance in this all too solitary place.

He continued staring at her with his dark, ferret-like eyes, as bright as if he had a fever. Emily glanced quickly around her, her heart racing and suddenly hoping Pino would appear out of the trees to rescue her.

"I'm not from here," he said to her in barely intelligible Italian.

The man had a kind of miniature barrel attached to a strap slung loosely across his shoulder. His dark shirt was roughly-made from what looked like sackcloth material. Every now and again, he would tug at the strap and move from one foot to the other. Emily was terrified, particularly when he came closer to her and muttered under his breath in an incomprehensible language; it sounded like he might be cursing her. What would happen if she pushed past him now and ran madly back to the house?

"I'm lost," he announced in Italian, pointing around at the tall trees. "Labyrinth," he added in what could have been Greek.

"Oh, I'm not from around here," she answered weakly. "Tourist."

"*Inglese*," he said, moving much closer and continuing to stare at her.

She somehow managed to blunder past him, but he was faster, grabbing her from behind, and she was immediately aware of a knife flashing near her face that made her blood run cold. Falling to the ground with a dull, heavy thud, she was abruptly face downward upon the cold earth, paralyzed with fear and only too aware of the man's hissing breath on her neck and his hard body against hers. She tried to scream but not one word came out. She closed her eyes – so this was going to be the end of her then, raped and cut to pieces in an Italian wood. Just as all these terrible thoughts were racing through her mind, there was a metallic thud from above her head and the man fell forward on top of her.

Pino suddenly loomed into sight. He was holding in his hands what must have been a spade that he now tossed over his shoulder with an air of nonchalance.

"You had a lucky escape there," he said curtly.

Emily managed to stagger to her feet, her eyes staring wildly and her lips parted in amazement.

"*Una punizione meritata*," he added, spitting on the ground near where the man with the knife now lay inert, blood oozing from his head.

"We must phone the police," she stammered feebly.

80

Pino looked sternly at her.

"No, no, there's no need for any of that!"

Beside the path upon which they were now standing, there was a steep embankment full of jagged rocks at the bottom. He nodded in its direction.

"Over there," he said.

The hard expression on his craggy, sun-blackened features convinced Emily he was going to do exactly what she feared.

He stooped down and rolled the lifeless body over a few times until it slid effortlessly down the embankment, far away and out of sight. Emily felt as if she was going to be sick. She checked herself as best as she could because Pino was staring at her once again with a peevish expression on his face. Then he trampled over the grass again to the very edge of the embankment. For a moment Emily thought he was about to slide down the slope after his victim.

"I've seen him about before," he said, turning back to her. "I don't remember exactly where I saw him – he wasn't from around here. Another *albanese*. One of Nino's shepherds perhaps. Nino is a very old friend of mine. I can tell him his shepherd has gone back to Tirana. No one will miss him, that's for sure."

Emily still looked blank and Pino turned away with a sigh. Shovelling up heaps of dry leaves with his spade, he threw them down the slope and then he got down on his hands and knees and carefully rearranged any tracks the body had made on the earthen path. When he stood up again, Emily instinctively took a step backwards.

"Well, I don't think you should be so very particular about a man like that," he said, starting to chuckle softly. At the sight of that ugly toothless grin, she had to resist an urge to run away. He must have guessed how she was feeling.

"You're out of your depth here," he said. "Go back to where you came from and forget all about this place!"

It was getting hot again even here in the shade and the bees were humming drowsily nearby, the cicadas strangely silent for once. Emily herself could hardly be bothered to uproot herself from where she was standing, mesmerised as she was by Pino's staring eyes. Suddenly she had the feeling she was about to fall over and she had to lean heavily against a tree.

"I don't want any police snooping around. It's as simple as that! No police!"

He glared at Emily, daring her to contradict him. He was a short muscular man but he seemed to increase in height as he spoke and Emily felt dreadfully conscious of being very close to the edge of the steep rocky embankment.

"Oh, don't worry," he said finally. "I'm not going to throw you down there if that's what you're thinking!"

He pulled in annoyance at the collar of his shirt, where his neck was looking red and chafed.

"You're not the way I imagined an Englishwoman to look," he said curtly. "It must be those clothes you're wearing."

Emily bit her lip, unable to speak.

"But it's the way you're looking at me that I don't like. You'd better forget about that man down there, forget what he tried to do and forget that I got rid of him for you. If you go talking, well, I can guarantee that's the end of your peace of mind. I'll be like a cancer in your side!"

Emily quickly shook her head.

"That's just as well then, since you rather remind me of an Irish girl I once knew in America. Well, she was prettier than you and she had lovely, copper-coloured hair:"

He sighed at the memory as he trod thoughtfully on a grassy patch at his feet.

"She had a strange name now – it sounded Indian to me, I can tell you. Milles, Mellot, something like that…"

82

He looked enquiringly at her.

"What do you think it was?"

"I don't know," Emily managed to stutter.

"Well, she sang like an angel out of paradise, I can tell you! Can you sing?"

She shook her head again.

Pino shuffled ever closer up to her; he lightly touched the frill on her sleeve, then he took a step back, took out a large handkerchief that he blew loudly into and dabbed at his eyes. Emily wondered what she could say. He looked at her now with his reddened eyes.

"I won't tell you all the terrible things that man's family have done to me, but you would surely pity me if you knew."

"Pity you…"

"*Santa Madonna*, I hate Toni Cellamare almost as much as I hated his father!" he exclaimed. "When we had to come back from America, we left everything behind. We were going to make a fresh start of it here… I suppose my poor mother thought she could tame that wild beast!"

Suddenly there was a rustling noise behind them and Chiara appeared out of the shadows, clothed in purple, looking not unlike some kind of pagan priestess, her beautiful dark hair arranged in luxuriant curls down her back.

"Well, well, and what a strange coincidence it is to meet one another in such a secluded place, far from prying eyes," she announced to Emily in her stilted but grammatically perfect English.

She graced Pino with a curt nod of recognition and he likewise bowed his head.

"I thought you had finally decided to move away from here, Signor Giocondo."

Pino remained utterly impassive, his craggy features hiding any emotions he might have been feeling.

"Anyway, the two of you look as if you're up to secret intrigues!" Chiara smiled thinly, enjoying the sight of Emily looking so flustered.

"Oh, I was just going back," she said, only too well aware of how dishevelled she must be looking.

"Surely you must know that our family has been in conflict with Signor Giocondo's for practically generations?"

"I suppose I did. It's nothing…" Emily left the sentence incomplete.

She had been going to say, "It's nothing to do with me", but Chiara's stern expression discouraged her from saying anything at all. Chiara Cellamare managed to make her feel idiotic as well as dull, just the way that Toni Cellamare did too, at least when he had been in his right mind.

"Are you in financial difficulties again, Signor Giocondo?" asked Chiara bluntly.

Although Pino still looked undaunted, Emily could sense a change in his mood and it made her feel even more apprehensive. She had no idea how she could get away. Just like her father again, Chiara had the ability to inspire subjection in people. Her pretty lips would curl up in that self-satisfied Mona Lisa smile just as she always managed to get whatever she wanted. Even Pino Giocondo had lost his laconic self-assurance.

"I should be getting back," said Emily quietly.

The trees obscured any brightness and the dim light that managed to penetrate the shadows only made the scene seem more ominous. If only Emily had never ventured into the woods in the first place.

"Let's walk back together then," said Chiara, much to Emily's disappointment.

She yawned with a great pretence at weariness as they said goodbye to watchful old Pino.

When they were once more in sight of the house, Chiara turned to Emily suddenly and spoke out with vehemence.

"Don't let him use you for his own ends. You know nothing whatsoever about that man!"

Emily was thinking of the tree-choked ravine as she glanced backwards at the gloomy thicket that had almost swallowed her up forever and shuddered involuntarily.

Ricky, who had been basking outside in the sunshine, smiled in delight at the sight of his girlfriend. Chiara immediately plumped herself down on the stone bench and began ruffling his unkempt hair.

"I went to the town to buy sausages," he said, looking lovingly at her. "I thought we could have a barbecue out here."

Chiara glanced at the uneven paving stones that formed a kind of patio where he had in fact managed to assemble a rusty old barbecue on its rusty old pedestal. Grapes had once grown on the trellis structure overhead, all that remained now, stark and desolately bare. Suddenly Grazia appeared out of the house, broom in hand and looking thoughtful.

"I'd like to speak to you for a moment if you don't mind, Chiara. It's about your father."

Very reluctantly, Chiara got up and followed Grazia into the house. Ricky finally seemed to remember Emily's existence.

"I thought you'd gone into town, you see. I was sure I'd find you there. It was rather busy today and there were even a couple of German tourists, would you believe? I don't know why but Germans always seem to get everywhere, don't they?"

Emily was silent. She did not know whether she should tell Ricky or not about what had happened to her in the woods that morning. She felt his eyes boring into her and she turned away from him.

"I don't like this way they have of taking people aside and having a quiet word. Have you noticed, Emily? Emily, I was saying, have you noticed? Are you all right?"

He stood up and came closer to her but Emily had already made her mind up; she wasn't going to tell anybody about what had happened to her. She had no intention of ever falling foul of old Pino who had told her not to speak about it. There was something about that old man which instilled fear in her.

"I found this old barbecue set this morning," said Ricky with a rueful smile. "I can't imagine who used it. I just can't see old Toni cooking a barbecue for his family – what a perfect family scene, eh! Here, come and help me and we'll have it going in a minute. We used to have barbecues in the back garden in Ireland when I was a kid. Great fun in spite of the rain!"

"Yes, but won't Toni mind?"

Ricky laughed.

"I don't understand the lot of you. Does Toni have such an effect on women? You're all so careful not to tread on his toes, as if he was a lord or something. Sir Toni, is that what we should call him?"

Emily smiled thinly and Ricky glanced at her.

"Well, and now you can tell me what's bothering you," he said.

Emily wanted to blurt out everything, but, instead of saying exactly what was haunting her, she said something slightly different.

"Oh, it's just like we're all in danger here. I can feel it in the air."

"So, Emily, you've suddenly realised your choice of friends has been unwise. A little too late, don't you think?"

"I'm all confused. I don't know what to do."

"Why did you come here at all?"

"Because Grazia asked me to."

"And you simply couldn't say no. No, of course you couldn't. Grazia was feeling pretty desperate and she leaned on you. She's very good at using people, isn't she? She's good at using me too."

He sighed heavily. Emily could not understand what he meant.

"Are you running away from something in Britain, is that it?"

Emily shook her head lamely.

"Why should you think that, Ricky?"

"Oh, it's what I've been able to infer from your behaviour. But, don't worry, it's the same for me. I shouldn't really be here at all. I shouldn't let old Toni order me about. It's a crazy situation. And the way they love to rake up old grudges. They've put themselves in this predicament and Toni's turned into a paranoiac – he thinks everybody's out to kill him now, not just the hit man on the bike!"

"He was almost murdered, Ricky, I was there. It was terrifying!"

"And maybe the hit man should have done his job a little bit better! Then we wouldn't be in this state of limbo, would we?"

It was Emily's turn to take a good hard look at him. She was on the point of saying something when Chiara suddenly appeared, sitting down beside Ricky with what seemed to Emily a very proprietorial air. She was carrying a tub of sun cream in one hand and she immediately began "anointing" herself – there seemed to be no better word for it – a simple gesture became a ceremonious rite when she performed it. Utterly mesmerised, Ricky watched her hand move rhythmically up and down her lovely tanned legs.

She apologised to him for leaving him alone so long, sighing regretfully as she spoke and staring at Ricky with such an air of intensity that Emily began to feel embarrassed.

"I'll just go and see if Grazia needs anything," she said, finding an excuse to leave them alone.

Chiara stretched out her long legs and blocked Emily's path.

"Why don't you make us a cup of coffee, there's a good girl! You can manage to make a good cup of *espresso italiano*?" she said, jutting her chin forward and squinting in the sunlight. "Grazia's in the kitchen, scraping the mould off the kitchen walls the last time I saw her like *un vero diavolo infuriato*!"

She began to laugh with Ricky and Emily left them both laughing their heads off. Grazia was indeed in the kitchen, together with Toni, moving a bulky cupboard with difficulty away from the wall. She was wearing a sleeveless polyester kimono and taking drags from a long slim cigarette from time to time. On the kitchen table, there was a large bottle of bleach and a plastic bucket. A single bare light bulb above their heads illuminated the scene.

"Not that we have any particular guarantee that I'll be safe here," Toni was saying as Emily came into the kitchen. He stopped speaking abruptly as soon as he saw her and stared at her in a way that that Emily found very disconcerting. Muttering some expletive or other under his breath, he sat down on one of the rickety kitchen chairs and looked peevishly in Grazia's direction; at least, he seemed quite subdued for once and not about to kick out physically at anybody. He was looking more and more like a down-and-out these days, having entirely lost that air of audacious panache that Emily had been confronted with in Rome.

Emily stepped forward quickly to steady a heavy cupboard that looked about to topple over on top of Grazia.

"Oh, Emily, you're here. I've been looking for you." She smiled graciously as she stubbed her cigarette out in a dirty cup. "We've been wanting to apologise for our recent behaviour. After all, we're really so glad to have you here with us, aren't we, Toni?"

Toni grunted something from his corner of the room and Emily was immediately filled with compunction at this entirely unexpected outburst of appreciation. She even decided there and then that she would tell Grazia what had happened in the woods that afternoon; she had to tell someone after all whatever Pino Giocondo said.

"I suppose you're wondering why we're moving the furniture about." Grazia paused for effect. "We want to substitute the old stove with something more modern, something that will actually work in the cold weather."

"What do you mean? For the winter?"

Grazia nodded and Emily felt her heart sinking. She had not been planning on spending the winter here, that was for sure.

Grazia continued cleaning the inside of the cupboard.

"Aren't you going back to Rome then?" Emily enquired.

Grazia simply shook her head and Toni giggled loudly as if Emily had just cracked a joke.

"We've decided to stay on here," said Grazia, looking complacently at Emily.

Emily moved a step back, inadvertently knocking a box of candles off the table. Toni reacted energetically, as if he had been lying in wait for just such an accident, Emily thought afterwards. Immediately he began to complain bitterly about Emily's clumsiness as he bent down to pick up the candles with a show of fussing over each one as if they had been so many babies.

"Look at them! Now they're all dented too. You see how you always manage to get in the way here! Always in the way, just like Enrico."

Grazia stopped short.

"Who's Enrico, Toni?"

Making a loud tutting noise, he turned away from them and pretended not to hear her continued entreaties. Emily glanced at Grazia and, suddenly, she could stand it no longer. Assuming an appropriately solemn expression, she coughed slightly, just enough to attract Grazia's attention.

"Grazia, I'm thinking of leaving. I can't be of any use here anymore."

"Whatever are you saying, Emily? Can't we talk about this later?"

"No, I want to speak now," said Emily, trying to keep her voice sounding calm. She really felt like screaming at the pair of them.

Grazia tried to placate her.

"Please don't go now. You can go next week or the week after."

"I'll leave as soon as I've packed my bag."

"Oh, I'm not ready for this," said Grazia, starting to whimper.

Toni rolled his eyes eloquently as Emily left the room and went upstairs. She felt as if a weight had just been lifted off her shoulders. It was now all a question of getting herself out of this damned house once and for all and as quickly as possible too. She had surely put up with too much already and she did not feel she could possibly be of any use to Grazia now.

There was a gentle knock on her bedroom door. Emily's heart sank.

"*Ciao*," said Grazia lamely. "Could I have a word with you? It's about Toni." She paused. "He isn't the same of course, you're aware of that. Don't worry, I won't try and persuade you to stay on here. There's no point in that, I suppose. I'd like you to get a message to Francesco. He's not answering my calls. You have to get him to come back here – he's the only one who'll be able to save Toni now!"

"I thought they didn't get on. I thought Chiara was his little darling!"

"Oh, yes. Chiara." Grazia heaved a deep, heartfelt sigh. "Toni hasn't always got on with Francesco, but only because of Francesco's decision to become a priest."

Emily wondered how the young priest felt, having to contend with such a father.

"Toni wanted Francesco to stay on here, you remember, and he refused to. Point-blank. Can you imagine that? Coming from a priest too!"

Emily shrugged her shoulders without making any comment.

"I'll keep in touch, Grazia," she said. "I'll send you letters at the post office."

She reached out and took Grazia's hand in hers, feeling a little sad and foolish at the same time.

"Thank you, anyway, Emily, you've been a calm quiet influence and I've appreciated your company, even if I haven't always shown my appreciation."

"Why do you want to stay on here?" Emily asked. "Why does he have to continue hiding?"

Grazia looked uncomfortable.

"I've agreed to stay on here for the winter, that's all. What else can I do? Better here than in freezing cold Milan – I'm not staying here forever, you know! I'll have to go back to a job sooner or later – this is only a kind of sabbatical."

"Oh, really, have you told Toni it's only a kind of sabbatical?"

Emily remembered all those heated disputes she had overheard them having not so very long ago.

"Are you going to have enough money to stay here over the winter?" Emily asked tentatively.

"Oh, money's not a problem, at least not for the moment. Toni's, um, alternative activities have put plenty of money in the bank…"

Emily mused over the meaning of this phrase.

"Alternative activities that might catch up with him eventually, you mean?"

Grazia spluttered, valiantly attempting to defend the error of her lover's ways before he had learned from the mistakes of the past.

Grazia even helped Emily take her large holdall downstairs. Ricky, in the meantime, had offered to give her a lift to the station. When she passed the kitchen, Toni was sitting tranquilly at the kitchen table, cutting up tinned tomatoes into a glazed bowl; he did not look up. In the gloomy hallway, Grazia gave her a letter, carefully enclosed in a white envelope and addressed to Francesco; she began to hunt around in her handbag for her address book.

"He lives not far from the *Colosseo*. Let me just copy down the address for you."

She wrote down the address on the envelope and gave the letter back to Emily.

"I hope you don't bear any grudges against Toni for his... behaviour towards you?"

Emily shook her head, kissing Grazia on both cheeks in Italian fashion, and walked outside into the sunshine. Ricky was standing outside the front door in front of the Vespa. He was just finishing telling Chiara about his crippled old grandmother in Omagh who drank Guinness at breakfast.

"She's in a terrible predicament, of course," he said in a fervent tone that surprised Emily. "They're going to put her in a nursing home – now that isn't right, is it?"

Chiara looked utterly unimpressed by his grumbling as she walked around the moped, swinging her shapely hips. She spotted Emily in the doorway and gave her a good long stare.

"Thanks for that marvellous double-roasted espresso, by the way, not that I was expecting you to hold the key to the secret of good coffee-making. *Figuriamoci!*"

Emily climbed on to the back of the Vespa in as graceful a manner as she could muster, gracing Chiara with a sort of smile and clutching her holdall for all she was worth.

At the station, where she was going to have to wait over an hour for a train, Ricky continued to glare at her.

"You're running away then," he said, finally breaking the silence.

"Wasn't that what you kept telling me to do, Ricky?"

"I suppose so," he said, stroking her bare wrist and standing close.

"I'll be in touch with all of you, Ricky, you know that."

"Oh, yes, a fat lot of use that will be. Exchanging letters wasn't really what I had in mind."

"What did you have in mind?"

Ricky hesitated for a fraction of a second, just the time it took for Emily's heart to miss a beat.

He bent down and kissed her very softly on the lips.

"There, I've been meaning to do that for a long time. It's too late now, though, isn't it? I'd been thinking you were just my kind of girl!"

With another shrug of his broad shoulders, Ricky got back on his Vespa and left Emily staring after him in wonder.

PART 2

CHAPTER 1

A FRIEND IN ROME

Francesco Cellamare stood in front of the first shelf, plainly entitled "ABC" in bold gold lettering, contemplating with misgiving the long rows of thick books in their shadowy recesses. He was never going to be able to read all of these. What was the point of studying all that philosophy in any case? Picking out a volume of Aristotle's "Ethics", he began leafing through it without much enthusiasm. He had just stopped to ponder over the meaning of the word *entelechia* when he was startled by a hearty pat on the back.

"I've been looking for you everywhere, Francesco. Don Valerio didn't know where you had got to and I didn't like to tell him why I wanted to find you!"

"Can you come to the point more quickly, Matteo?"

Matteo frowned and leaned over to whisper something in Francesco's ear that was impossible to catch.

"What on earth are you being so secretive about?"

"A woman has come here looking for you. Quite attractive too." He uttered this adjective in the same kind of breathless way another person would have said the word "naked" or "pornographic".

"You must be sensible about this, Francesco," he said, raising his thick black eyebrows that met in the middle over a bulbous nose. "I didn't realise you were such a daredevil. Don Valerio will find out about your goings-on, you know – he always does. No, no, the previous fellow apparently turned a blind eye to what the novices got up to. He considered such things *bricconate* but not Don Valerio. He has testified against his fellow priests."

Matteo looked so scandalised by what he evidently considered the man's lack of loyalty to the priesthood that Francesco was on the point of defending his spiritual advisor. He glared at Matteo but Matteo did not even seem to notice. Francesco hated having to share a room with him, particularly since it meant Matteo could pretend to be on really familiar terms with his roommate. Francesco could not understand why someone like Matteo, a young man with no ideas of his own and certainly no particular vocation, had any desire to become a priest. His mother wanted him to become a priest, he had said to Francesco once, and it had evidently not occurred to him to question her wishes. Matteo was very good at cutting remarks: he had something to rebuke all the other novice priests for. On any number of occasions, Francesco could have quarrelled with him about his malicious tongue but he ended up keeping his resentment to himself, quickly learning to avoid Matteo as much as possible. He went to bed late and got up early in the morning before Matteo did. Fortunately, Francesco had discovered one advantage in their ground floor room; he could look out of the large bay window that overlooked the courtyard and see who was entering the building. If he saw Matteo, he had plenty of time to get out of the bedroom they shared, walk quickly down the corridor in the opposite direction to the paved courtyard and very often out into the street, where he would have to resist an impulse to run. He had even started avoiding the communal refectory for fear of bumping into Matteo.

Francesco could barely hide his irritation now at the expression on Matteo's face, beaming with malicious contentment. How he would enlarge and add to the news of an attractive woman asking for him. Perhaps Matteo would try to have him expelled from the seminary; he would certainly enjoy that.

"Where is this woman now?" he asked in a deliberately flat tone of voice. "Perhaps it's my sister."

Matteo chuckled.

"Oh no, it wasn't your sister. I've met your sister, don't you remember? No, this woman isn't quite in your sister's class. Well, she's older, more mature, I mean, rather dejected in her manner. I thought perhaps unsettled by a love story gone wrong."

He stared at Francesco, scrutinising him carefully for a reaction to what he had just said.

"Oh, it would be perfectly natural, Francesco," he added with that conspiratorial air that distinguished him. "We surely all have something to hide here."

Perhaps Matteo finally realised he was irritating Francesco because his face assumed an expression of holier-than-thou wisdom and he began looking carefully along a line of books. Matteo felt superior to the other novices; he had been brought up to feel like that by his pious widowed mother and his two maiden aunts in Siena. As a schoolboy, he had been one of the contestants in a very well-known TV quiz show, his team somehow managing to win in spite of all his mistakes. He still called it the crowning moment of glory of his boyhood and it had, for ever more, inflated his already exaggerated sense of his own importance.

"Well, where is she?" Francesco insisted, still trying not to sound overly interested.

"Oh, downstairs in the long corridor."

Francesco left Matteo leafing through a gilt-bound prayer book, a smug expression on his face. He entered the gloomily-lit hallway in search of his visitor. Emily was certainly not his idea of a seductress and he could not for the life of him imagine what Matteo had meant when he imagined Francesco falling under her spell. The "enchantress" turned around at the sound of his footsteps on the flagstones.

"Pleased to meet you again," she said, shaking his hand a little limply. She handed him a small envelope; he sized up the handwriting before opening it.

"So they're sending you to do errands now, are they?"

Afternoon sunlight filtered through the Venetian blinds and formed luminous stripes on Emily's cotton skirt. Francesco read Grazia's letter, nodding now and again and noting she had not signed it.

"She values you very highly – I bet you didn't know that! 'One of the most exceptional teachers I've ever encountered,' she says here."

Emily did not particularly appreciate his amused expression as he read out these compliments, smiling to himself.

"Excellent teacher," he continued to quote. "She's already mentioned that surely… Why does she have to keep repeating the phrase? I don't own a language school, do I! Oh well, I suppose she just likes flaunting such a learned friend."

He stuffed the letter roughly back inside its envelope and looked her straight in the face with those disarmingly beautiful dark eyes.

"When I first met Grazia, she was living in the centre of Milan, Emily – I can call you Emily, can't I? You know what she's like in any case. I just can't imagine her, of all people, continuing to live there in such straitened circumstances."

"I think she wants you to go there, I mean, rather urgently too."

He indicated a couple of chairs in a small room off the corridor, its walls embellished with any number of portraits of elderly prelates from centuries gone by, and they sat down, Emily gratefully sinking down onto the cushions and feeling that nobody was ever going to be able to uproot her.

"She wants me to go back there – it's not my favourite place in the world, never has been – all falling down and desolate in the middle of nowhere. I don't know why my father didn't sell it years ago."

Without Emily noticing, someone had placed two glasses and a jug of ice-cold water on a little table in front of them. Emily sipped from the glass that Francesco poured out for her and admired the view of distant Roman rooftops. She was delighted to be back in Rome, pleased too that she was still able to recognise so many odd corners of the Eternal City and not just the sights visited by the tourists either. She rejoiced to see still familiar restaurants that had not changed their names. Piero had liked one in particular near St. Peter's and, with the dashing arrogance of youth, had always called it by his own name so that when she had passed it today, she remembered it as *Da Piero*. She had wanted to go inside and ask for him after all these years. He might still be sitting in their usual corner, staring at the little vase of plastic flowers, and just waiting for her to come through the door after another business English lesson. In those far off days, she could hardly cook – toasted cheese maybe – and he could make nothing at all, apart from coffee. He used to buy bags of coffee beans and ground his own special blend in an antiquated machine that had probably belonged to one of his ancestors. What good coffee though – if she closed her eyes, she could almost conjure up the aroma.

"I wonder what you must have thought of my roommate, Matteo – I believe he has relatives in England so he can speak decent English."

Emily smiled shyly; she had not noticed anything about the young man except perhaps that he was more like her idea of a priest than Francesco Cellamare, who was obviously far too good-looking.

"I feel I should make up for the time you've lost on running errands for my family," he said with a winning smile. "Let's go and eat something."

Perhaps she should have said no, but, as things turned out, she found herself very soon sitting at a polished table in a restaurant near the seminary. Francesco was ordering Sicilian wine from the wine list. Grazia's letter was on the table beside his empty glass.

"Don't think what's in this letter doesn't distress me! I still love my father, of course, in spite of his behaviour, but I can't help him."

Francesco sipped the wine that the waiter had by now poured out and looked directly at Emily. She moved uncomfortably on her chair and waited for him to continue.

"He tried to prevent me from entering the priesthood. I didn't get one lira from him. I had to go begging around various institutes."

He stared unhappily into his wine glass. Emily glanced across at Francesco's lean, handsome face, noticing for the first time a small birthmark where his wide forehead met his thick dark hair. She could not imagine him ever having to beg for anything.

"My father's been frightening everybody down there, has he? I can just imagine it!"

"No, I don't think you can. He isn't like his old self at all – that's why Grazia wants your help. He's… depressed or something… such strange behaviour. I mean, one minute he's knocking down doors, the next he can't drag himself out of his bedroom. Grazia can't cope anymore!"

Emily had raised her voice and a group of well-dressed Italian businessmen turned to stare in her direction. They seemed to find seeing a young attractive priest in the company of a foreign woman a very amusing spectacle.

"Why do you all think that I can save him? Why me? No, no, don't say anything! I know the answer already – you think that just because I'm a priest I can always find the solution – well, I'm sorry to have to disappoint you. I've not been freed from my human characteristics yet – who knows, perhaps when I die and they make me a saint, I can intervene to save my father's soul!"

Emily suddenly felt terribly weary; she wondered whether her legs that were feeling so heavy would be able to take her back to the unprepossessing hotel she had found near the station. Francesco glanced across at Emily, irritated by her silence. He hardly knew what to make of this pale, thin foreign woman. She had looked so surly the first time he had met her, but he now realised he had misjudged her. She appeared quite meek and defenceless, sitting in front of him now; her bare arms could have belonged to a child.

"I feel exhausted," she said finally and he thought she looked close to tears. "It feels like I haven't had a shower for days – I really think I should just go back to my hotel."

"Where are you staying?"

"The Hotel Principe – sounds grand, but it most definitely isn't – just something I found up a side street from the station."

He immediately looked concerned.

"Oh, I could find a room for you in one of our Catholic Association hostels – lovely clean rooms…"

"No, no, don't worry about me. I'm of good constitution, I assure you. I can cope with the Hotel Principe."

"No, no, I insist."

"No, really, it's not as awful as all that! Come and see for yourself…"

"So that my roommate would have something to talk about! He's the kind of shallow-minded hypocrite who lives for such details. Gossip and chocolate cake under the bed – a heady combination!"

The waiter arrived with bowls of soup. It made such a pleasant change to Emily's recent diet of constant pasta that she could not refuse to eat it.

"This looks good," said Francesco. "It's called *pappa col pomodoro* – I hope you like tomatoes. You see, the cook comes from Florence and he believes it's his job in life to cook only Tuscan specialities for the tourists in Rome. I think it's like a form of propaganda for his hometown!"

"Surely there are enough tourists in Florence as it is," said Emily, smiling at her own memories of traipsing around the famous city on a trip she had taken there with Piero.

"Of course there are, but that's Italians for you. Each of them firmly believes their own town is the best – it's called *campanilismo*."

"Well, perhaps he's just homesick and he finds some comfort in cooking the dishes his mother used to make."

Francesco looked curiously at Emily for a moment.

"Where are you from, Emily – I mean, originally?"

"Oh, my parents moved about a bit. In England, mainly, but we stayed in Glasgow for all of four years in a row too. Very near the university. My father's job meant he was always being moved about the country so we had to go along with him every time that happened. My mother was a very tolerant kind of woman."

"And why are you here in Italy? "

Emily looked flummoxed and fell silent. Why indeed?

"I came out here to see Grazia. We've known each other for a long time and I suppose I just wanted to come back to Italy, that's all. I used to work at a language school in Rome, you know."

"Is that where you met Grazia?"

Emily shook her head.

"My grandfather was Italian and we're kind of related."

They fell silent. Emily was thinking of the phone call she was supposed to be making that evening, of Grazia shrieking down the phone at her when she told her it was no use; Francesco was not going to help. She looked at him as he was eating his soup. The artificial light reflected off his shiny black hair and emphasised the perfect line of his middle parting. Perhaps she was at fault, she thought; she should have begged more, pressed him more, and continued to nag him in some way? Why shouldn't he be able to help his own father?

"Chiara's still there, you know, has been all this time," she said slowly.

She watched the smile freeze on his lips. He broke a breadstick on to a side plate and tapped the crumbs.

"You never mentioned that."

"I thought you knew. She came down with Ricky, don't you remember?"

"*Per amor del cielo*, not that wretched fellow," he blurted out.

"Why do you say that? Don't you like him?" asked Emily, somewhat bemused.

She was thinking how peculiar it was that a brother and sister could be such exact opposites: Chiara all extravagant pouts and frills and Francesco who was moderation itself.

"I can't say I know him that well," he said, resuming a ponderous tone of voice again. "I mean I don't even see very much of my sister these days. We were quite close before, you know – she almost had a breakdown when our mother died. My father was no use at all!"

"Oh, I got the impression she didn't get on so well with your mother."

"Really, is that what she told you?"

"Oh, no, it was probably something Toni said."

"There you are then. My father says a lot of things that aren't true. My mother was a saint, the way she managed to put up with him for the sake of the family."

His voice became louder and he had begun to gesticulate, not very unusual for an Italian but certainly unusual for Francesco.

Suddenly Emily felt more exhausted than ever and she ended up begging him to take her back to her hotel. He promptly called for a taxi and said he would ring her at the Hotel Principe if he managed to find her alternative accommodation.

CHAPTER 2

AT THE LAKESIDE

The car made a peculiar rumbling noise going through the tunnel. Emily hated tunnels on motorways and there were so many of them here in Italy, interminably long ones where enormous lorries thundered past at an alarming rate. She had rented a car for the weekend and was feeling much the better for it in spite of the strain it would put on her finances. The ring road was busy as it always was – she was heading north of Rome on a trip down memory lane that she had been unable to resist. The lake was in front of her now, looking as smooth as the proverbial millpond, and Piero's hometown was on its northern shore.

Emily drove around the lake, barely aware of the sunny day and the beautiful panorama, until she had actually reached the little town of Trevignano Romano where she parked near the shore and walked across the road, looking out for any familiar landmarks. Where was his uncle's *pasticceria*, the place that had always been their first stop whenever they went back to visit Piero's hometown? The gorgeously-decorated windows with their tiers of inviting cakes had been replaced by a garish-looking supermarket. She read the name – *Testa Discount* – in large black letters. She went inside, bought herself a packet of *torrone* and asked the cashier what had happened to the *pasticceria*. He could not have been more than seventeen years of age and had never heard of it. How she would have liked to ask him about Piero Nisi and the rest of the family, but she hesitated a moment too long and he turned his attention to other customers.

She remembered all the fuss of her leaving. After a suitably banal argument, she had gathered her belongings together in a very dramatic huff, leaving poor Piero in a pathetically tormented state. Of course she had been so young back then; perhaps she should have taken more time over such a momentous decision, but she had always done things rashly, one of the very reasons she had come back now. How wistfully she could recall Piero's downy cheeks, his handsome face with its rather solemn expression and his dark brown eyes full of love for her.

He had been one of her students; that was how they had met. She could still remember how lost and helpless he had looked at his first English lesson, practically trembling whenever she asked him a question. He was a hopeless student, one of those who thought they could pass exams simply by copying from the others. Perfectly open about this, he had told her this system had always worked for him before and was genuinely surprised copying was not allowed at Emily's language school in the centre of Rome. He even had a degree in something or other. Evidently, his university teachers had not controlled the exam halls very well, crammed as they would have been with scribbling students all copying furiously from one another.

They had lived together in a rented flat on the ground floor of a suitably ancient, decaying building a stone's throw away from the Fontana di Trevi; it had suited her taste much more than his. All the Italians she had met then aspired to owning modern houses with gleaming white, wall-to-wall formica in practically every room – a style she herself could not stand. She liked a faded, genteel look in an old house with plenty of room for cats. She loved animals and could hardly see a stray cat without wanting to pick it up, to Piero's barely disguised disgust, and she had ended up sheltering a few of them in their flat where they would curl up on the windowsill, awaiting her arrival as surely as Piero did. He used to plead with her to get rid of them, at least when his mother was due to visit.

"Why do all these creatures congregate at your door, Piero? You must be feeding them!" Her round red cheeks would noticeably inflate whenever she got annoyed about something.

"Not at all, *mammina cara*," Piero used to lie, while Emily would be asking herself when his mother was leaving.

It had been with a passion verging on obsession that Emily had detested her prospective mother-in-law, the most bigoted and snobbish individual she had ever met in her life. Poor Piero had lived so much in awe of her he would sit bolt upright whenever she entered the room if not actually jumping to attention. She had what Piero lovingly referred to as *un naso importante* – a nose so imposing it always reminded Emily of a toucan's beak – and very thick hair of an improbably golden sheen that she used to fluff up whenever she wanted to catch people's attention. She was always immaculately dressed, managing to display an inordinate quantity of jewels at any time of the day or possibly, Emily suspected, also at night. Sometimes, Piero would tentatively mutter something in Emily's ear about her dress sense or, rather, her lack of it, suggesting to her it was about time his mother took her in hand. But Emily had not the slightest intention of looking as if she were constantly dressed for a board meeting nor had she any desire of encouraging the "feudal lord" manner of his mother: she had, in a word, rebelled. When she had left him, Piero's mother had probably had the bells of their local church peeled in gratitude.

There it stood now in fact, set back from the shore on the hillside, looking exactly as she remembered it: *la chiesa di Santa Maria Assunta*. She looked around for the workshops of his family's leather business but they were again nowhere to be seen and she began to feel restless. Why on earth had she come back here? All at once she loathed herself and this chronic inability she had of leaving the past well alone.

Black clouds were gathering on the other side of the almost completely circular Lake Bracciano, forty miles from Rome. Bad weather approaching, she thought, imagining herself driving back to her hotel in a thunderstorm. The outlying hills were already hidden by clouds yet it was still oppressively hot in the little lakeside town. Emily began to walk slowly down the street, past the information kiosk in the square, to her parked car. She threw a backward glance at the shimmering lake as if to say goodbye to it forever.

"Buongiorno, signora, non ci conosciamo?"

Emily turned around to find a handsome young man, alert-looking husky at his side, smiling down at her.

"I'm Giorgio Lanzillotti, Piero Nisi's nephew. Don't you remember me?"

The memory of a sunny day in May and a boy's First Communion came suddenly flooding back. She was surprised that this young man with his fashionably cropped blond hair and designer sunglasses should remember her at all. They were standing in front of what must have been a cobbler's shop – there was no shop sign, just piles of old-looking shoes in the window and an old man in a grubby plastic apron, sitting on a stool at the open door, smoking a cigarette.

"It's a beautiful spot for a holiday, isn't it? Are you here with your family?" he asked her, politely removing his sunglasses.

Emily looked evasive. She nodded vaguely; she didn't feel like telling him she was actually single and childless.

"And what about you, Giorgio? What do you do now?"

"Oh, I'm a *geometra* in Viterbo but my wife likes to visit her parents in Rome every weekend. That's where she is at the moment." He looked rather glum as he said this. "Her father works in the film industry, so she would like me to work with him. She wants me to make more money."

108

Emily sensed his smouldering resentment and changed subject. She found herself unable to resist asking Giorgio about Piero Nisi.

"Oh, don't you keep in touch? Zio Piero left Trevignano a year or two ago. He lives in Germany now."

Emily was completely taken aback.

"What's he doing there?" she asked, trying to make her voice sound as casual and disinterested as possible.

"Well, he went there to see the World Cup, you see, and managed to find a job, a good job too. He works for a pharmaceutical company, I can't remember the name. He lives with a German woman he met in Frankfurt. Her name's Ulrike and she looks like a top model."

This last revelation hit Emily very hard and she had difficulty forcing her face to assume an unnaturally passive expression.

"It's an on and off sort of relationship, she told me," Giorgio went on, happy to chat. "You remember my mother, I suppose, and Zia Isabella – he keeps in touch with them, of course."

Emily didn't like to admit to only very vaguely remembering Giorgio's mother, only one of Piero's innumerable aunts. Isabella was a different story though. She had been in her last year at school when Emily had been going out with her brother. She had come to stay with them in Rome any number of times, reporting every detail back to her mother and there were always plenty of details – the awful clothes Emily wore, the way she got up late for lessons and had to rush around in the mornings, leaving dirty dishes in the sink, even an apple core on the sofa. (How uproariously appalled had Piero's dreadful mother been by this last revelation.)

"Zia Isabella is a very attractive woman now – she's married to an accountant and they've got twins."

Giorgio was evidently in no hurry to go home; he liked to talk so much Emily only had to nod her head now and again. Finally, he gazed at her with his green eyes, speckled with gold, as if he were seeing her for the very first time.

"Time for coffee, don't you think?" he said.

She nodded her head.

"Shall we go in my car? It's an Alfa Romeo," he added proudly.

"Oh, we can leave the car. Let's go on foot to that little bar on the lakeside, the one with all the ivy-covered arches. It must still be there."

There were quite a lot of people enjoying the autumn sunshine; young soldiers in their khaki uniforms on leave, mothers pushing prams and old couples walking their toy dogs. Apart from Giorgio's marvellously well-behaved husky, there were never any dogs bigger than a Yorkshire terrier or a Chihuahua. She saw the bar next to the horse chestnut tree, its thick foliage looking very golden indeed in the afternoon sunlight. A gentle breeze blew the leaves, making some of them fly off and land on the surface of the lake. The bar itself looked so very different that at first Emily thought they must have pulled down the original building and rebuilt it. She remembered dark-coloured booths where she and Piero had been able to hide. Now it was all a kind of extreme open-plan arrangement inside as well as outside where there were white plastic tables and chairs with whitewashed brick walls. She looked over towards the lakeside tables where at least the ivy-covered arches were just the same; she had used to sit there with Piero, holding his hand and talking about honeymooning in Paris. It could all have happened yesterday.

The barman must have been a friend of the family since he started asking Giorgio all about the lot of them, while he offered them both slices of homemade tart made with grape jam.

"Whatever happened to Piero Nisi?" inquired the barman suddenly. "I haven't seen him around here for years.

Emily stared at him for a moment, trying to associate this well-dressed middle-aged man with a shining bald head and expanding waistline with a younger long-haired version wearing ragged jeans; she gave up trying and he certainly didn't recognise her.

"He must be about my age of course. Woken up to reality now, I suppose!" The barman sighed. "We all felt like masters of the world back then."

He handed them chocolates from a pannier next to the cash till and steadfastly refused to accept any payment for their coffees.

Giorgio walked her back to her car.

"I've got a screen test coming up – they might have me in the latest edition of *Grande Fratello*," he said, looking extremely pleased with himself.

"*Grande Fratello*?"

Emily looked astonished; "Big Brother" was certainly the last programme she would ever watch on TV and she could hardly imagine anything she would less like to do, for all the prize money in the world.

"Why do you want to do that, Giorgio?"

He was taken aback by her lack of enthusiasm for what was evidently one of his dream projects.

"It'll be fun being in a house with people I don't know. And even if I don't win, I might still get noticed by a 'talent scout'." He used the English expression with a certain relish, deliberately emphasising every syllable.

"I'm afraid it's not a situation I'd like to find myself in. I like my privacy too much."

"Of course, you are English."

Giorgio smiled knowingly. As far as he concerned, that fact alone explained a whole lot of peculiarities.

One of the straps of Emily's light cotton dress had fallen of her shoulders. Giorgio stared at it for a second and moved a little closer.

"I still don't understand why you wanted to come back to Trevignano after all these years."

Emily blushed.

"Oh, you know, I was in Rome. It was like I had to make this little visit to the lakeside."

She looked over in the direction of the lake, as if staring fixedly at it might convince Giorgio of the truth in what she was saying.

"Are you still teaching English then?"

"Well, not just at the moment. I was working in London."

Giorgio nodded knowledgeably. He had been to London more than once.

Emily had finally found her car keys.

"Take care of yourself then," he said, stretching out his hand towards hers and leaning forward for the customary goodbye kiss.

Falling leaves had collected on the car bonnet. The wind lifted the long brown hair hanging loose over her shoulder. Suddenly she did not want to say goodbye to Giorgio so abruptly; it was as if her only link of Piero and her past life was about to be broken.

"What about if I come back here again?" she said. "We could meet up, couldn't we, Giorgio?"

The young man's eyes immediately brightened.

"Of course, of course! I'll give you my phone number – my mobile, of course."

He winked at her, looking forward to the prospect of what he evidently imagined was to be an assignation. The hopeful hangdog look on his handsome face suddenly reminded Emily of Piero and she felt like she was going to succumb to a bout of tears. She held out her hand to him and was surprised by the firm way he held on to it.

"You're the most beautiful Englishwoman I've ever met," he said.

She wondered how many Englishwomen he had met in his life – he was probably comparing her favourably with some old hag at his secondary school. She was aware of the limits of her faded charm, but she still managed to feel flattered by his compliment and was glad that fate had somehow thrown them together. The husky at his side, so well-behaved up until now, barked up at them and their prolonged handshake. This moment of intimacy was suddenly shattered by the sound of a piercing voice behind them – even the dog looked cowed. Emily was speechless and, for a moment, she thought she must be dreaming. Piero's mother was bearing down upon them, even more barrel-shaped than Emily remembered her. Looking extremely upset, she harangued Giorgio for ten minutes without interruption until, finally, turning around to face Emily. Only very gradually did it dawn on her just who this pale, thin woman was.

"Oh, it's you," she said at last, unable to find anything else to say. Not another word came out of those thinly-puckered lips.

"Yes, I'm in Rome again," said Emily, who likewise could find nothing better to say. What she would have liked to say was quite different: "You sent me away, you ruined my life, and you are responsible for all these years of solitude!"

In the meantime, Piero's mother had apparently forgotten all about her and had turned her attention back to her errant nephew. Evidently used to hearing his imperious aunt order him about, Giorgio was looking suitably contrite.

"Wilma has refused to come to eat dinner with us on Sunday. Is your wife completely mad? She actually said she couldn't cope with an entire afternoon in our company, can you believe that? Those were her very words!"

Signora Nisi still bristled with outrage at the memory of that morning's phone call.

Good for Wilma, thought Emily to herself. Why hadn't she done the same all those years before? Why hadn't she fought back against the woman's insidious malice?

"I hope you'll get through to that wife of yours that she cannot treat her husband's family in this way. She isn't respecting you either, Giorgio, when she acts like that!"

Emily had imagined the woman was going to ignore her presence entirely but it was not to be. She suddenly turned her full attention back to Emily, the sunlight glancing off the lenses of the large glasses she now wore, making her dark gimlet-hole eyes suddenly loom very large indeed.

"Well, it's a funny thing to see you again, I must say! You just disappeared without a word, didn't you! Piero had a hard time back then. Of course, the poor lad managed to get over it all fast enough!"

She smiled with satisfaction as she said this, leaving Emily entirely incapable of speech, and glanced back at Giorgio, who was now moving from foot to foot and looking very awkward.

"I want you to agree to Sunday dinner, Giorgio. You can go home and inform your wife about her obligations towards your family."

"Can't we forget about this weekend? I mean we can always come *un'altra volta*."

"Another time indeed!" she scoffed. "Zia Tramis is planning to visit us. She's coming over from Canada and they're renting a car to come up to Trevignano. Surely you want to see her?"

This was indeed a historical event. Piero's aunt from Canada, his great aunt, to be exact, had been old enough even back when Emily had been living with Piero all those years before. The woman was a bit of a celebrity in his hometown; Francesca Tramis had just so happened to be in Dallas the very day President Kennedy was assassinated. Piero used to joke that it had been Zia Tramis who had pulled the trigger. He had so much wanted Emily to meet her one day.

Signora Nisi suddenly laughed and ruffled Giorgio's hair in the way that an affectionate aunt would.

"You've always been a terrible rascal, Giorgio, but I know I can depend on my favourite nephew!" she said. "*A domenica allora!*"

This completely unarmed poor Giorgio, who began to look more sheepish than ever. Piero's mother even graced Emily with a benign expression, shaking her head slightly and bestowing on her a sweeping glance that somehow managed to convey her scathing opinion of Emily's scarecrow-like appearance, as if it was on account of that very appearance that she was unable to invite her to come to Sunday lunch too. Emily did exactly what she had done before; she bowed her head as of old and soundlessly said goodbye to both Giorgio Lanzillotti and Piero Nisi.

CHAPTER 3

AN ENGLISH GENTLEMAN

Back at the hotel was a brief letter from Grazia, telling Emily all about Toni's latest antics, how he continued to play with his cavalrymen and continued to bark at them all as if they were staff under his military command. Now and again she even managed to go down to the village when Ricky and Chiara agreed to stay behind with Toni; she said it was like changing the guard every time. Never away very long, she would come back and find him in his usual corner, absorbed in playing with his cavalrymen. Occasionally, there would be a row with Ricky; Toni was convinced that, whenever he left the room where the toy soldiers were kept, Ricky would creep in and move his musketeers about. It would all have made Emily smile if not for the thought of poor Grazia having to put up with his strange behaviour. Ricky liked to wind up Toni; whenever he came back from the village, he would make up reports of bands of *mafiosi* hanging about street corners and asking him about the precise whereabouts of Toni Cellamare. Toni was terrified out of his wits.

Emily, in the meantime, had been deliberately vague about Francesco's intentions and had somehow managed to raise Grazia's hopes with her very vagueness. In fact she seemed to be expecting Francesco to arrive any day now and save the situation. Emily hugged a quilt around her legs and put the letter down with a sigh. Although she had not spelt it out as such in her letter, she could sense Grazia was floundering.

Emily's dingy hotel room was practically opposite one of Rome's lesser-known theatres. A crowd of people were now emerging from the foyer, doors wide open to the magical Roman twilight, neon sign twinkling attractively in the dusk. It made her think of all the times she had gone to the theatre with Piero, who used to complain about her going on and on interminably about the delights of Shakespeare.

Now she could hardly think of anything except Grazia and the fear she felt for her, living in that remote sinister place with a maniac. There, she had finally let her thoughts find the right word. Toni Cellamare had gone mad. He would end up killing somebody. How on earth could Grazia put up with it? Someone would have to do something. She would have to go and speak to Francesco again.

When Emily got into bed, she tossed and turned for ages, eventually falling asleep and dreaming about cliff top edges, masked hit men on mopeds and, strangely enough, her Italian grandfather from Tuscany, long since dead, who suddenly appeared in her dream and saved everyone.

***

Rather theatrical in his movements, Mr. Pickett, director of the Shelley School of English, arrived late for his appointment with Emily, raised his hat at his two secretaries before taking it off with a graceful flourish and warmly shook hands with this latest applicant for a teaching position. Emily settled into a plush velvet chair and enjoyed the full attention of his olde-worlde good manners. The dark-haired secretary with the bright pink hair band winked conspiratorially at her before setting a steaming cup of tea down in front of her.

117

"You'll love working in this school, I'm sure of that. I think of my staff as members of my family!"

He beamed at her and rattled on about the joys of teaching "the glorious English language". He was evidently in his element and gesticulated possibly even more than all the Italians Emily had ever met.

Glancing out of the window, she could just make out the Ponte Sant'Angelo spanning the Tiber and the honey-pale castle itself rising majestically above its esplanade. Her heart suddenly stirred at the sight of 2000 or so years of history.

Mr. Pickett was talking about how he formed the various English courses in his school and Emily continued to glance, surreptitiously, out of the window. A couple of stray cats were foraging in a dustbin when a beagle, pulling hard on its leash, suddenly appeared from around a corner and made them scamper away.

"I had a business partner, you know, Italian in actual fact, but he was a complete scoundrel – left me with a lot of debts!"

Mr. Pickett had grey hair he kept tossing back with one hand, but, every time he threw it back, a little cluster would somehow manage to evade him and fall forward on to his heavily-lined forehead.

"Now you told me on the phone you speak Italian – always a plus having a bilingual teacher, you know."

Emily nodded her head in what she hoped was a non-committal way. She felt herself being attentively observed by one of the secretaries, the more elegant one with the large silver earrings and the sleek black hair tied back in an intricate knot worthy of a top hairdresser.

"This partner I had, well, he's now opened another school in what is practically a neighbouring street – can you believe that?"

Mr. Pickett put that bony hand through his hair again, his lips pursing and a worried expression stamped on his face. He got up at last and walked Emily to the door.

"Another couple of teachers will be arriving from London very soon and we'll be able to see about finding a flat for all of you. Last year, they rented a flat just over the river – hardly a stone's throw from the school in fact and very handy for them. Now my name's Bill, by the way, no formality here, you know!"

A crushing handshake had left her bones feeling numb as she sat down at a nearby bar where a nun and her charge of little girls in pink smocks were choosing ice creams from a vast assortment behind glass counters. Emily noticed that the people bustling past her were already wearing smart padded jackets and, unbelievably, ankle boots. She looked down at her bare legs and open-toed sandals and remembered that, whenever Grazia had wanted to criticise her, she would just say Emily dressed like *un'inglese*.

Sifting through the sheaf of papers that Mr. Pickett had given her, she read all about the various English courses on offer that all made the Shelley School sound like the best place in the whole wide world for learning English. All this publicity even made Emily happy to think she would soon be a part of it, particularly when she looked up and could just make out the imposing bulk of the Castel Sant'Angelo across the river. Autumn leaves lay scattered at her feet and she continued to linger, entranced as she was by the mere fact of being back in Rome.

At last, she put a hand through her dishevelled hair and set off smartly in the direction of her hotel, scattering the dry leaves at her feet. Narrow streets crammed with all kinds of shops and restaurants branched off every road she took, each one jam-packed with parked cars and scooters. A modern statue embellished the white stucco entrance to the Hotel Principe or, at least, it usually did. Emily stared blankly at the stone fragments scattered on the ground. Some vandal must have lopped off its head, or so she supposed, until she saw the front door of the hotel, hanging off its hinges. One of the windows had been smashed in and the hotel manager was in the process of covering it up with a makeshift board. Trailing his customary whiff of expensive scent, the handsome little Sicilian turned around at her approaching footsteps, flung away his cigarette in the gutter and smiled benignly at Emily as if what she was seeing was all in the line of duty. He might very well have been related to the portly proprietor of the *Forchetta d'Oro*. Two policemen blocked her passageway.

Onlookers had gathered outside the hotel and Emily recognised two or three familiar faces from the local shops. The usually solemn-faced lady from the shop that sold the smelly cheeses Emily detested was chattering gregariously to the fat heavily made-up woman, who was normally perennially immured inside her overflowing newspaper kiosk on the corner, where an incredible assortment of colourful magazines and dailies were thrown together, apparently at random. They both nodded at Emily as if she were an old acquaintance.

She continued staring incredulously at the remains of the column that had once stood beside the door, its Ionic capital lying forlornly on the marble steps beside the charred embers of what must once have been the window frame. There was a gaping hole in the wall through which Emily could see bits of chairs lying around on what was left of the flooring.

The fat lady sidled up to her; she was munching Pringles crisps from a long tube.

"They threw a bomb," she announced suddenly between mouthfuls. "They could have killed somebody!"

Emily thought she looked a little disappointed; a death would have meant television cameras and a few moments of celebrity for the lot of them.

A young seminarist was standing near them, staring openly at Emily and making comments to a freshly-tonsured young monk standing at his side. The sight of them started the newsagent chatting about her two younger sisters who played the guitar in a church band in Civitavecchia.

"Do you know that priest?" she asked. "He keeps looking straight over here."

Emily had noticed too; it had gradually dawned on her just where she had seen him before: Francesco's roommate, the one he was always trying to avoid

"Well they're certainly going to have a lot of difficulty clearing up everything for the guests. The Germans will make such a fuss." She looked hard at Emily. "You'll have to sleep somewhere else tonight, *mia cara*."

The hotel manager was now speaking to a policeman; he held a piece of paper in his hand – Emily thought it might be a list of furniture and fittings that had been damaged in the explosion. The hotel staff were being allowed back into the hotel in dribs and drabs and a carpenter arrived with his tool kit on hand, ready to repair the window frame.

Suddenly the hotel manager came straight over to Emily. He was looking a little embarrassed.

"Would you mind if I have a word with you?" He nodded at the newsagent. "In private."

He led her over to the policeman, who introduced himself in good English with a benevolent smile. A middle-aged woman with copper-coloured hair was standing two metres away, scribbling things down in a notebook. The newspapers would publish their one-sided version of events. She could just imagine it all. She would be identified as some kind of suspect and Mr. Pickett would then tell her that her services were no longer required at his prestigious institute.

"Signorina Crespi, I would just like to ask you a few questions." He smiled encouragingly at her. "Perhaps you could just give me a brief summary of your stay here in Italy. I believe you've been here some time, am I correct?"

Emily nodded in a vague sort of way.

"And do you know a man called Dottore Antonio Cellamare?"

Emily's heart must have stopped. She was unable to say anything; she was aware only of an incessant throbbing in her head and two large black eyes behind gold-rimmed glasses

121

peering at her. The hotel manager's face loomed large in front of her. Shaking his head at the policeman, he looked ruefully at her. Emily had never noticed before just how small his eyes were and how red his large nose was. The pretty receptionist had once let slip he kept a bottle of port under his desk for medicinal purposes.

"We have two lines of enquiry," continued the policeman, nodding his head in the direction of the hotel manager who was now whispering in the ear of the pretty receptionist. "You know how things sometimes work in Italy. This is an area where people have to pay what is called a *pizzo* to the local gang. One of the gang members was seen here the other evening. He was probably acting like a "tax collector", if you see what I mean. When they don't get paid quickly, they put a bomb through the window as a warning."

Emily looked suitably incredulous and asked him why the police could not put a stop to it.

"Oh, nobody will ever admit to anything of the kind. The manager denies it, of course. As I said, that's one of our lines of enquiry."

"And the other one?"

"The hotel received a rather cryptic fax this morning and your name was mentioned in connection with Dottor Cellamare as well as the certainty of a bomb attack. Fortunately, nobody has been injured this time – the bomb may have been intended as a warning to someone. We're trying to discover who that somebody is."

He looked darkly down at her, all powerful in his dark blue uniform, and started asking her all kinds of information, managing somehow to sift through the vague details she so unwillingly gave him.

"So his woman friend is actually related to you in some way, is that right? And you don't know where she is presently?"

"No, I have no idea."

He looked at her for a moment, his dark eyes boring into her in a way she could not stand, before scribbling something down in his notebook.

"Well, we may yet discover that this nasty business had nothing to do with you or your... friends. As I said, there may well be a local gang to blame – what they call *una resa dei conti*!"

The crowd outside the hotel had diminished considerably; they must have lost interest in the gaping hole in the wall and the ground littered with assorted debris. The hotel manager had raised his voice and Emily could hear what they were saying.

"You can't treat me like this, Carlo, after all we've been through together!" the receptionist said in a tearful voice.

Emily raised her eyebrows and the policeman looked up from his notebook where he had just finished scribbling.

"I don't want to trouble you, of course, but I would like to ask you not to leave Rome without first informing us."

"Oh, I haven't got the slightest intention of leaving Rome. I'm starting a new job on Tuesday."

"Where are you working?"

"At the Shelley School of English. You're not going to say anything to them, I hope?"

"*Non é necessario*," he replied, checking over his notes and finally letting her go.

They all went on foot to a nearby hotel where the manager had found rooms for everyone until the Hotel Principe was in business again. There were lots of soldiers in khaki uniforms milling around outside; the barracks were just around the corner. The tenants of the building next door to the hotel had even come out to have a good long stare at the dozen or so guests from the Hotel Principe. News travelled fast and arrived very often in one distorted form or other. Emily was asked if it were true that a million euros had been stolen from the hotel safe. She shook her head.

Hard to believe but the Hotel Belvedere made the Hotel Principe appear positively princely in comparison, judging from the peeling plaster on the walls and the threadbare faded carpet in the hallway. There was no lift; only a long, winding staircase and what looked a total scarcity of even the minimal comforts that the Hotel Principe had offered its guests. Emily went up to her tiny bedroom on the fourth floor that boasted a fine view of a very narrow back street, wondering with a sense of foreboding what other mishaps could possibly befall her now.

CHAPTER 4

A SURPRISE VISITOR

Bill Pickett was glued to his computer screen that morning, not in fact perusing his favourite pornographic site but a website all about new quarantine regulations in Britain. He was thinking of going back there very soon to visit an ailing aunt and had no intention of leaving his pet parrots behind, however vexed he was upon discovering just how expensive it was all going to be. He suddenly felt himself being stared at and turned around swiftly just in time to catch sight of Monica averting her gaze.

Once upon a time, the idea of having two pretty young secretaries had thrilled him but certainly no longer: there was nothing remotely sexy about their relationship with him. They always seemed to be secretly intriguing together and they would often fall silent abruptly whenever he walked past them. Monica would throw him a deprecating glance that left him in no doubt as to just what she thought of him – a slovenly old relic straight out of the dark ages, one who should at least be carried about on a sedan chair and certainly not in any modern form of transport. Her boyfriend always came to pick her up in a shining silver Alfa Romeo that he double-parked outside with unnecessary panache and a lot of noise. He would be wearing dark sunglasses that he never took off even when it was raining. Sabrina was older than Monica but just as obsessed by her looks, possibly more so. Mr. Pickett had often caught her fiddling around either with nail polish or with a pocket mirror and eyebrow tweezers when she should have been typing out the obligatory class registers. Appearance was everything in Italy, as Mr. Pickett had discovered to his cost. In this country no amount of hard work was ever going to compensate for his gawkiness and lack of charm.

Turning aside from the computer screen, he smoothed out the newspaper on his desk and began scanning the various headlines: the usual nonsense about the Italian treasury being down in the doldrums, an overly large article about a royal wedding in Sweden (who was interested in these people, Mr. Pickett wondered), more illegal immigrants being picked up in the Channel of Sicily (the royal wedding was more interesting than that surely) – all in all, a pretty ordinary day in the history of the world. Energy crisis – well, that was one headline he could do without. He was going to have to sell his car at the rate things were going, though even that would be a makeshift solution. How much would he get for a ten-year-old Ford Escort with ample evidence of careless driving? There had been a period of his life when he had driven a second-hand silver Mercedes, but he had managed to crash that. An accident that could easily have had him losing his nerve as well as his life but, in fact, he remained indomitable behind the steering wheel, incapable certainly but inescapably enthusiastic. He had discovered that one of the joys of living in Italy was that he was able to do practically whatever he liked with his car. If he had been driving in Britain, they would already have given him a prison sentence. His Italian wife had divorced him on account of his erratic driving or, at least, that was what she had claimed. He had not been overly upset in any case, having had more than enough of his venomously malicious mother-in-law, a woman who would probably have been burned at the stake for sorcery in another epoch. She would have despatched him off to Hell in a trice. Thank God that period of his life was over – he had not the slightest desire to see his ex-wife or her family ever again and he tried his very best not to pay any alimony. Again he could do this in Italy. It was all on account of a son he had supposedly conceived when he was still married to Marina. He knew fine well that this son was not his but he was still legally obliged to provide for the boy, whom he saw extremely rarely – a quiet, drippy teenager with dark oily hair that left stains on his car upholstery. Bill Pickett was not of a paternal frame of mind, he had rapidly discovered, particularly when he recalled to mind that Gianni was actually the fruit of an illicit union between Marina and the plumber (possibly), the next door neighbour (much more likely) or the very handsome furniture shop salesman (almost certainly) who had been delivering a new kitchen in that period. He had caught them kissing behind the unfinished wooden partition of one of the kitchen cupboards; it had been the last straw as far as he was concerned even though it was actually Marina who had packed a couple of suitcases and left them for him in front of the lift, changing the lock of the front door while she was about it, probably all with the help of the obliging furniture shop salesman and his tool kit.

Bill Pickett's "senior teacher" (as he liked to call her) had just come in and was stooping over some boxes of newly delivered textbooks that she began stacking into neat piles. Bill observed her surreptitiously; Rosemary had been working at his school for the past four years and he was in love with her. He immediately noticed a coffee stain on his shirt and began rubbing at it without success. Such were the trials of being in love. He stooped under his desk where he managed to comb what was left of his wispy grey hair. She moved calmly from one textbook to another, entirely unaware of the deep sentiment she had provoked in her employer's aging breast. She would have thought it was a joke if someone had suggested the very possibility of her boss being in love with her, particularly as she considered Bill Pickett a very peculiar man indeed, still more so when he began stuttering painfully whenever he uttered two words to her. Monica, of course, had immediately guessed the cause of her employer's gibberish-like stammering and had quickly informed the other secretary. They had giggled long and loudly; they had laughed almost as loudly when they had found out the meaning of Rosemary's surname – Slaughter. *Massacro rosmarino* was what they called her behind her back – "the rosemary massacre".

Students were beginning to converge in the hallway and winsome Rosemary Slaughter moved amongst them; she was wearing a short-sleeved blouse that showed off her lovely bare arms and gently sloping shoulders.

"I hope you'll forgive me saying so, Rosemary, but you're looking l-l-l-ove-ly today!"

He had finally managed to blurt it out all at once, practically without a stutter. Unaware of the feelings hidden behind such a banal compliment, Rosemary smiled vaguely and carried on chatting to one of her teenage students.

Monica, who was busily putting make-up on, paused momentarily and turned to Sabrina with a dramatic flourish, trying to imitate Mr. Pickett's excessive height and gawky manner.

"*Troppo comico!*" she said as she quoted what she had just overheard. "You're r-r-really looking l-l-l-ove-ly today!"

Sabrina glanced at Mr. Pickett, looking more woeful than ever, and giggled.

A young man with a bulging rucksack on his shoulders had just walked in and was now lounging about in the waiting room with all the semblance of somebody feeling very much at home. When the school bell went off, signalling the beginning of the lesson, he barely looked up. As far as Mr. Pickett was concerned, it always sounded ominously like an alarm bell, still managing to make him jump after all these years. Disheartened by the pile of bills that had accumulated on his desk in his absence and feeling subdued on account of Rosemary's evident lack of interest, he looked out of the window at the groups of schoolchildren forming outside the secondary school on the opposite side of the street. As a schoolboy himself many moons ago, he had wanted to become a pop singer or an actor. He had even toyed with the idea of becoming a priest because he had imagined himself becoming a bishop or an archbishop, wearing bright red robes and a colourful mitre on his head. He still saw them in Piazza della Minerva, those wistful seminarists admiring golden mitres in the windows of ecclesiastical outfitters. Somehow or other, he had ended up in Italy, attracted by its ancient history and one too many adventure stories of standard bearers in far-flung Roman legions. Whenever he could manage to be completely alone and undisturbed, he lay down on the sofa in his flat and watched "The Gladiator," for the umpteenth time, and dreamt he was in fact Russell Crowe. He rather envied those young men around the Colosseum who were actually being paid to dress up as legionaries for the tourists.

Even the furnishings in his little flat just off Trastevere reflected these tastes; it was full of antiques he had picked up for a song in the many antique markets he had visited in the Lazio region, a plaster cast bust of Julius Caesar on the mantelpiece, a nineteenth century print of barefoot friars wandering around the ruins of the ancient Forum, a painting of the Madonna (of the Neapolitan school) above his bed. He dedicated his prayers to her every evening, what with there being so many things he had to ask her forgiveness for.

Apart from the secondary school on the opposite side of the road, he had an ample view of the busy crossroads on the corner. The sun was shining brightly in that pitiless way it only shone in Rome and he turned back to his desk. At that moment he finally caught sight of Ricky Brown in the waiting room, his lank hair and generally unkempt appearance contrasting oddly with the pristinely tidy waiting area. Bill Pickett's heart had begun to beat very fast. He sat down, slightly comforted by the fact that there was a flimsy wooden partition hiding him; Ricky could not have seen him yet, he was sure of that. He popped his head above the partition, glanced quickly at Ricky and sat down again. The young man did not look particularly menacing – in fact, he was looking rather melancholy, repentant perhaps. Bill Pickett could not decide what to do. It all depended on Ricky's intentions. Had he come back to carry out what he had threatened or had he returned to plead for forgiveness? He dismissed this latter possibility as extremely remote.

At that very moment, Emily walked into the entrance hall. Needless to say, she got quite a fright when she saw Ricky sitting there. He jumped up from his seat when he saw her.

"Go on, admit it, I bet I was the last person you expected to see!" he announced with childish fervour, so unlike the way she remembered him that she was unable to put up any resistance when he hurried forward and hugged her.

"Has something happened, Ricky? Don't tell me you're here on your own?"

Emily imagined he had come to bring her tidings of disaster.

"On my own and staying that way! I had quite enough of Toni Cellamare, I can tell you, the old bastard!"

"What about Grazia, Ricky? How is she?"

Ricky fell silent and Emily began to feel worried. She noticed the way Ricky was looking more unkempt than she remembered him, his hair standing on end and his bony face unshaven.

"It was an unpleasant situation for everybody and I'm out of it now! Even Chiara – well, it's like the spell's broken, that's all!"

He looked down at his steel watch, expensive-looking and not at all in keeping with his general appearance.

"That looks new, Ricky," she said, without thinking.

"And new it is," he replied. "A parting gift!"

"From Chiara?"

Ricky mumbled something Emily could not catch.

"I've just seen the weather forecast in the paper," he said, changing subject. "We're going to be getting colder weather very soon."

He produced a packet of chewing gum out of a voluminous pocket of his oversized jacket.

"Can we go back to your place, Emily? I thought I'd stay in Rome for a bit until I can think straight again."

"Well, I don't actually have a place as such, Ricky. I'm in a hotel at the moment – it's a real hole, actually! I'm supposed to be starting teaching tomorrow…"

Ricky smiled.

"Congratulations – you'll be earning some money! I was thinking I could find some bar work. Speaking of bars, why don't we go to the one across the road right now? We deserve a drink, don't we, for the summer we've been through!"

Emily looked unsure.

"I was going to go over my course books this morning. I'm teaching tomorrow."

He took her elbow gently.

"Come back later then. Who's stopping you?"

He smiled in that appealing way he had and she found herself gazing into those grey eyes again.

"Is it really all over between you and Chiara?" Emily was finally bold enough to ask.

"Of course it is. We were arguing all the time, don't you remember?"

Emily could remember nothing of the kind but she followed him in any case as he went down the stairs, two steps at a time.

Bill Pickett stole a glance at the waiting room and breathed a heartfelt sigh of relief. He had looked for a moment like someone going to his death and now he felt suddenly euphoric, as though he had just been granted a repeal of his sentence.

CHAPTER 5

THE CUPOLA

It had certainly not been Emily's idea to climb up the steps of St. Peter's all the way up to the top of the cupola; she had always been a little frightened of heights so she had to keep reminding herself not to look down. The view of Rome was magnificent in any case. They had come up with a group of Japanese tourists, all chattering amicably in their incomprehensible language, who rushed over to the parapet as soon as they could, in what seemed to Emily an excess of enthusiasm. To be on the safe side, she held back against the wall, gazing down at the famous square through half-closed eyes. Ricky shook his head at her.

"Why didn't you tell me you don't like heights?" he said with that half-smile he had, ruffling her hair gently and making her heart beat very fast.

He finally kissed her and she no longer cared about the bystanders, her arms hanging limply at her side as he pressed against her, blinded by the dazzling rays of the sun. When someone started shouting and yelling near them, Ricky broke away from her. It was only a group of teenagers arguing, laughing, carrying on or whatever it had been, enough to break that magic moment.

"I can't make you out at all, Ricky," she said. "I think your mind's still on Chiara, isn't it?"

At first he said nothing, just wrinkled his brow and stared at the purple scarf around her neck as if mesmerised by it.

"Chiara's got other things to think about…"

Emily waited, expecting this mysterious phrase to lead up to some more intimate disclosure; it was not forthcoming.

"Let's go back to my hotel – it's getting too windy up here," she said.

"We could wait for the sunset up here. Wouldn't you like that, Emily? We'd be entirely alone once this crowd go away."

Emily was far too conscious of being hundreds of feet above the ground far below and she shied away from going anywhere near the railing.

She could hardly believe all Ricky's little attentions, the way he would hold doors open for her with an ever so gentlemanly flourish or close windows because she felt the cold. Altogether too good to be true and she still wanted to know what had happened to Chiara, who would certainly not have let him go without a fight. Or had she found someone else? Something about the way Ricky avoided looking at her whenever Chiara's name was mentioned made her doubt he was telling her the whole truth.

Having insisted that lone sunsets far from the madding crowd were not her cup of tea, Emily had finally got her way and they were now walking under the embrace of Bernini's colonnade, watching life in the piazza, the tourists taking pictures of the mighty obelisk and solemn priests hurrying across the square with their heads bent.

"What's going to happen now in that house?" she asked him, trying to draw him imperceptibly into a discussion of how things were going to turn out for poor Grazia now, on her own with a lunatic.

"Oh, they'll be all right without our help, Emily," he said, lowering his eyelids and adroitly changing subject yet again. He began talking about his possible return to Ireland in the near future and what did she think of going on a trip to Donegal with him.

When Emily finally walked into the small cramped space that was, in actual fact, the hotel lobby, arm in arm with Ricky, the night porter had just started his shift. Taking off his reading glasses all the better to scrutinise them, he looked Ricky up and down from top to toe.

"Can I be of any service?" he asked in his heavily accented English.

He put some letters away in a drawer that he locked with a large key he then began to twist in his plump, fleshy fingers while he continued staring at them with beady eyes. Ricky merely tucked his forearm under Emily's in an unmistakeably proprietorial way, staring shamelessly back at him before giving him a knowing wink that, to Emily's horror, the oily little man, twitching his bulldog jowls, promptly returned.

Ricky immediately appeared very much at home in Emily's bedroom. He picked up her Freya Stark travel books from their shelf and wandered idly around the room before going out on to the tiny balcony where he descried the "riff raff" loitering in the hotel courtyard. He then complained bitterly about the deadening noise of traffic when he opened the other window that faced the main street.

"I want something to eat," he said, picking up the phone and asking for room service that Emily was surprised to discover actually existed in this lowly hotel. "Not a bad room you've got. Is it expensive?"

Emily gazed at the vine-leaf pattern of the wallpaper and explained about the bombing incident at the Hotel Principe. Ricky nodded sagely, as if nothing would surprise him any more in Italy.

"Well, this place sounds much better. Ideally located for sightseeing too if you had a mind for it. You only need to turn the corner and you're in the centre of Rome – almost!"

Emily was not entirely convinced, but she was too taken aback by the dawning realisation that they had little to say to each other now that they were no longer trapped together at the old farmhouse, where they had somehow felt linked by a country and language they happened to have in common. Ricky had now become too pale and emaciated even to be considered handsome any more. Why had she ever found him attractive?

There was a knock at the door – a dark-skinned young man, little more than a boy, carrying a tray of sandwiches and a plate of what looked like a jelly trifle. He placed the food on the low table next to the bed and waited there expectantly, a tentative smile on his face. Ricky ignored him adroitly and Emily was obliged to get out her purse.

"Now let's have a better look," said Ricky, opening the sandwiches and discarding the lettuce leaves he found, without a thought to Emily. "Tell the guy we want a couple of beers while you're at it – Italian beer will do fine."

Was it really possible that his presence had already begun to pall? Her voice took on a peevish note that Ricky pretended not to notice, even though he was perfectly well able to deduce the change in Emily's mood.

It had suddenly got much windier, the leafy branches of a sycamore tree outside flapping noisily against the window and the rusty hinges of the window shutters creaking in true horror-film-like fashion.

Ricky had finished eating at long last. He looked at Emily with a wry expression on his face and pointed to the luridly green couch near the window.

"I can sleep there, you know – it looks comfortable enough."

Emily nodded without adding another word.

CHAPTER 6

THE PROFESSOR

Bill Pickett lived on the first floor of a block of flats opposite a one-time building site that had gradually turned into a desolate wasteland of weedy refuse, ever since the builders had been put on trial for embezzlement. An old man, bent double, was regularly to be seen there, gathering the plants of *cicoria selvatica* that grew between the unfinished or, more appropriately, 'un-started' blocks of cement. It was a rustic dish that even Bill had come to appreciate, at least when it was made by someone else. He was entirely uninterested in cooking; yet another of his myriad faults as far as his ex-wife was concerned. His mother had once kept various pots of herbs on the stone steps leading down to the back garden; even now the lemony scent of sorrel, the fragrance of basil, rosemary and sage would bring back childhood memories – his mother tending her plants with more attention than she had ever dedicated to her sons, headstrong Aaron who later emigrated to Australia, and timid William. Bill's father had died when he was eight, which was just as well, he sometimes reflected, considering that the most vivid memory he had of him was of a large, bristly man chasing him around the kitchen table with a fishing rod in one hand, with which he had been intent on beating the living daylights out of his younger son as his wife cringed in a corner of the living room. Bill's mother, on the other hand, may have had her faults but, as a boy growing up, he had adored her together with the extravagant plumed hats she wore to church on Sundays and the way she would sing her off-tune imitation of Shirley Bassey in the bath every morning before going off to yet another coffee morning with her twin sisters, Aunt Gloria and Aunt Gladys. How he had loved hanging around her and her bejewelled, vivacious friends with their bright red nails, loud voices and bags of peppermint creams at the ready.

The biggest disappointment of his life came the day he found his mother's arms entwined around the man who was later to become his stepfather. "Go on", he used to say to Bill at dinnertime as he forcefully shovelled fruit chutneys and revoltingly hot mustards into the little boy's mouth. "Be a devil, there's a good boy!" When Bill did not behave himself, he would tie his stepson's hands together with strong twine he kept for that purpose in the garden shed, in true Dickensian melodramatic style. But Bill Pickett was able to smile about him now that he was in an old folks' home in Brighton. Neither Bill nor his brother ever visited him now that his mother was no longer alive.

The parrots squawked on their perch, their exotic colour contrasting starkly with the shabby squalor of Bill's kitchen with its flaking walls and dirty dishes, heaped up higgledy-piggledy in the sink. Living on his own had made Bill unsociable; he lived like a hermit when he was no longer behind his desk at the language school.

Standing at the window and making a half-hearted attempt at clearing away some of the dishes, Bill waved back at the old man gathering weeds in the glare of the afternoon sun. Who would ever have thought that this man had once taught science in one of the best secondary schools in Rome? He would probably still be teaching there now had somebody not chanced to inform the authorities about the marvellous get ups he used to wear of an evening whenever he went out on the town, and he always did use to go out on the town, get ups that would include leopard-print mini-skirts, stiletto heels and fishnet stockings. Now he looked neither like *il professore* nor any more like a cross-dresser, his face unshaven and his thick woollen vest, which he wore even in the height of summer, quite visible under a grubby checked shirt. Apparently, he had been grief-stricken when he had lost his teaching post, but nobody could have imagined those sentiments now, looking into his old lined face, the very picture of serenity as he wandered from one clump of grass to another.

Bill got the bowl of sugar down from the cupboard and poured himself out a cup of Darjeeling. He did not have to wait long for the doorbell to ring. Clutching a plastic bag that was full of wild chicory leaves and rocket as well as a cracked terracotta vase of basil, the *professore* immediately sat down at Bill's kitchen table, a seraphic look on his pale face.

"I was actually just on my way out," Bill instinctively lied, getting down another cup all the same.

"Oh, you wouldn't want to miss these," said the old man. "Very pungent, just the way you like them. I could set up a pulley system at the window, you know, ever so easy."

"I could as easily lower a basket," said Bill. "You don't need to go squandering your scientific skills on me – save them up for someone else."

The old man smiled in that vague, dewy-eyed way he had, the same vacant smile that so put off passers-by at street corners. Not very long ago, he had been punched on the nose by a drunken teenager who had taken offence at that very same smile.

The old man upset the cup of tea that Bill set down in front of him at the table. The hot liquid spilled on to his trousers and he jumped up quickly, taking them off without a second thought. It struck Bill as somewhat indecent – the sight of this old man, thin white arms akimbo and a vacuous expression on his face, standing forlornly in his kitchen in his vest and underpants. Politely averting his eyes, he picked up the cracked cup and mopped up the tea.

"I ran into Professoressa Porpora the other day," the old man said, a touch of sadness in his voice. "Quite by chance, you know, the supermarket on Via Portuense, and she ignored me."

"Who is she?" asked Bill.

"The headmistress at my old school," he said, staring hollow-eyed into the cup of tea that Bill had newly placed in front of him. "I should never have been treated like that."

"Perhaps she didn't recognise you."

"Oh, I didn't mean that – I'm talking about the way the school directors treated me. I didn't commit a crime!"

With the old man's appraising eyes upon him, Bill, horribly ill-at-ease, could not think of anything whatsoever to say. He found the very idea of men wearing make-up and women's clothes unsettling, to say the least. One of his neighbours had even told him that *il professore*, whose hair had once been naturally strawberry blonde, had looked pretty stunning dressed up as a woman, in his heyday.

All that was very difficult to imagine now, Bill reflected, as he surveyed this wreck of a human being, hair awry, fretfully rubbing his liver-spotted hands together and railing against his unfair dismissal. Bill moved uncomfortably on his chair and said a silent prayer to send his guest away, but the old man's eye had suddenly been caught by the sight of plastic shopping bags, emblazoned with the name of the discount supermarket where Bill did his shopping. He looked stricken.

"You too! Do you see where we have to shop – cheap and nasty, that's what I say, but I can't afford any better nowadays!"

He stopped his tirade for a moment to fiddle with his gums and Bill watched in horror as the old man's hand disappeared entirely into the darkness of his mouth.

"This biscuit's too hard for me," he said at last. "I have to buy the soft variety these days. Oh, how I used to love eating *torrone*! My mother would make it from our very own almond trees – the best in all of Puglia. You should have seen those trees in bloom. *Che bellezza!*"

The old man's presence was already beginning to weary Bill and he wondered how he could ever get rid of him.

"Well, I suppose I should be going – I have classes to arrange."

"But it's Saturday. I thought you said your school was shut on Saturdays. I remember you telling me once that your teachers would never tolerate having to work at the weekends."

"Of course, that's basically the idea, but we sometimes have lessons on Saturdays," Bill lied.

In the meantime, the poodle of his next door neighbour, with whom he was on appalling terms, had begun to howl relentlessly and Bill silently cursed it; he had never liked dogs. He did not like his neighbours either for that matter. How often would Signora Licola scream at her various family members, without the slightest regard for Bill, who had, on any number of occasions, been woken up by either their irate voices or by the incessant noise of their ghastly heavy-metal-playing teenage son, the one who unfortunately reminded him of his very own Gianni Pickett.

The *professore* suddenly changed tack, as was his wont, and began imploring Bill for a loan. Bill would have liked to just tell him to go to hell in no uncertain terms, but he loathed the idea of being considered a skinflint or a lout, for that matter. In the condominium, they were already quick enough to say bad things about *l'inglese* behind his back.

"I have a lottery ticket, you know – I'll give it to you. It's bound to win – they're numbers that appear to me in my dreams!"

He got up and walked over to the window where he peered out with vacant eyes from behind the flimsy curtains and put a wrinkled hand on the windowsill to steady himself. Only then did he seem to realise he was still in his underpants.

"Oh, you must think me very ill-mannered! Don't you have anything for me to put on?"

Bill got up and went over to the laundry pile to vainly search for a pair of tracksuit trousers. The *professore* took this as an opportunity to slip his arm through Bill's in an unpleasantly confidential manner.

"May I offer you my undying affection, Bill?" he said, using his Christian name for the first time.

Bill felt a little like pushing him to the floor. All he actually did was to sit down at the table again, his eyes fixed on the man's large gnarled hands. He gulped down what was left of his tea and tried not to take any notice of the frayed shirt tails that were flapping around his skinny white thighs. He was reminded of a creepy old man who had used to hang around on the corner outside the private boys' school his mother, with more money than sense back then, had obliged him to attend.

"I had an English lover in the good old days, you know," continued the professore unabatedly. "His name was Fuller. I remember him very well – he used to like reading Milton to me. 'Paradise Lost.' He was the one who felt he'd found paradise!" He roared with laughter at his own silly little joke before falling silent again and slumping down on to a wicker chair at the window.

"Then he began to plague me with phone calls – oh, something like 40 a day. He was jealous, you see!"

To Bill's great distress, the *professore* was evidently in his element talking about his sentimental adventures.

"He gave me lots of presents too. I have a wardrobe full of Armani clothes, quite as colourful as those delightful parrots of yours, you know. You should come up and see them some time."

Bill was beginning to feel menaced by the man and poured himself out yet another cup of tea that he quickly gulped down while being thrown amorous looks. The old man began to sing softly, half under his breath, and Bill quickly realised it was some kind of grotesque variation of a Neapolitan love song, albeit performed in a squeaky tone of voice that certainly did not do it the justice it deserved. He had become uncomfortably aware of the old man's tight-fitting underpants. He would certainly set all the neighbours talking if he threw him out in his underwear. How on earth was he going to get out of this predicament?

"Well, would you like to come back to my flat then to look at my beautiful ornaments?"

It was all too much for Bill. He finally stood up and marched over to the door.

"Now look here, I don't want to have to quarrel with you, but I think it's high time you went home!"

The old man continued smiling.

"Oh, don't worry, I won't bring you to ruin. I'm very discreet, you know."

He got up purposefully and sauntered over to Bill, who, to his own utter dismay, found himself now feeling strangely, but not unpleasantly, perturbed.

"I used to have a villa in the countryside… I had to sell it, of course, to pay off a debt." He paused, suddenly forgetful of Bill's proximity. "I come from a very small town in Puglia. You wouldn't know it, nobody ever does – I haven't been back for over twenty years."

"Don't you still have family there?" asked Bill, his curiosity aroused in spite of himself.

The old man looked sadly down at the floor.

"I've got two sisters, Elisabetta and little Lucia. I haven't seen them for years and years. They haven't wanted to speak to me ever since my career was ruined. I miss them so much!"

He burst out crying as soon as he said this. Bill actually managed to forget the vicinity of the man's bare legs and patted the man's back in the charitable fashion that his mother would have been proud of.

"They're the ones who spurred me on in the first place. I never would have become a teacher at all if it hadn't been for them!" He gazed into the distance. "I can only afford to live in a hovel nowadays. You've no idea – it wasn't always like this."

He became quietly self-absorbed, sitting down again and laying his head on the table. Bill felt sorry for the man.

"You'll be all right," he said in order to comfort him.

What was really extraordinary was the fact that it was not an empty phrase at all. Bill was really thinking of helping him out. First of all, he would just have to cancel his imminent flight to England.

CHAPTER 7

THE UNWELCOME GUEST

Emily peeped into the tiny room where the curtains were still drawn. Ricky had been asleep on the sofa for the last twelve hours. She could only manage to surmise from this that he had not been getting much sleep recently at the farmhouse. She went over to the window, making as little noise as possible, and opened the shutters slightly. Ricky did not stir at all. Emily wandered out on to her little balcony; it overlooked an internal courtyard and was eerily empty for the time of day apart from a couple of cats lapping up milk from an enormous tin bowl.

Emily was thinking about how to get rid of Ricky. She rehearsed what she was going to say to him when he woke up. Of course, when he did finally wake up, she said nothing of the kind.

"I'm just on my way to the school," she said, hoping that he might add he was leaving that very morning.

Ricky nodded sleepily in reply and asked her where she kept her shampoo and whether she could get somebody from the bar to send him up a cup of coffee.

"Are you thinking of going out later?" she asked him in a faint voice. "I won't be able to stay in this hotel much longer, you know…" She broke off, waiting for his reaction.

He said nothing whatsoever. In fact, he didn't pay her much attention at all as he leant over to switch on the TV.

"If you can just tell somebody down at the bar about that cup of coffee – a cappuccino of course, and maybe something to eat. Nothing fancy… and nothing with jam. I don't like jam much."

Emily nodded meekly.

The Hotel Belvedere was a maze of corridors and doors. A baby was wailing in one of the rooms, a dog was whimpering in another and the flimsy wooden partitions that made a kind of TV room on the large landing shook with the rumble of traffic outside. She hated everything about the place – its cracked walls with their peeling plaster and the creaking floorboards on the steep staircase that led down to the "reception desk", if she could give it such a grand title, where the manager or whatever he was would squirm uncomfortably in his chair whenever Emily asked him anything. When he was not sitting there, there was a thickset woman who sometimes took his place. She would sigh and frown and look darkly at the hotel guests as they scuttled past, usually as quickly as possible. She stared at Emily now, somehow managing to express displeasure with a heave of her large breasts. In one corner of the cramped reception area, an elderly woman in a flowered dressing gown was lulling a baby to sleep in her arms. A little girl moved restlessly on the chair next to her. Finally, she stood up abruptly and went over to a rickety bookshelf, where she stared at Emily. She had copper-coloured hair and very pale skin and Emily imagined she must be foreign until she opened her mouth to speak rudely to her grandmother in the thick accent of a real *trasteverine*.

"*Signora*," the receptionist called out as Emily walked past. "*Qualcuno ha telefonato per Lei.*"

Emily asked if this person had left a name. She had not. Had the woman said she would phone back? The stout receptionist, looking a ghastly wan colour in the artificial lighting, shook her head.

It was impossible to get any more information from her so Emily simply shrugged her shoulders.

"*Un cappuccino nella stanza 103 per favore,*" she added.

Raising her thick eyebrows, the woman shook her head yet again and told Emily peremptorily that there were currently no bar staff.

Emily walked out of the place, feeling worn out before her day had even begun. She decided to take a different route to the school so that she could stroll along the leafy banks of the Tiber. It was a quiet street she had turned into and her heels made a loud tapping noise on the uneven cobblestones, littered with brittle yellow leaves, as she looked around for "accommodation to let" signs. Finding a decent flat, relatively central and above all cheap, was not going to be an easy task, but she had decided she was going to make a clean break with the past. Working hard – that was going to be the way forward from now on. The moment might even have arrived for her to think about going back to Britain – it was time she sorted herself out. This love affair with Italy truly had to end. Grazia would have rolled her eyes and made disparaging remarks about Emily's general cluelessness. She worried about Grazia. Had Grazia phoned her at the hotel, trying desperately to get in touch with her? What would she be doing now, alone with a madman, in the sweltering heat of the south in an environment that was so totally alien to her? She should be sitting on a metallic bar stool, sipping a cocktail, inside the sophisticated glassy precincts of the Galleria Vittorio Emanuele in her native Milan, probably running down Emily to her glamorous friends, as she had done so blithely in days of yore. As she was busy musing upon her troubled relationship with Grazia, Emily became suddenly rooted to the spot as she caught sight of a familiar-looking face on the opposite side of the street. She looked back to make sure and saw her again – Chiara

Cellamare, silky dark hair tied back in a chignon and wearing one of her favourite purple blouses, walking briskly along the pavement on the other side of the street. This unexpected apparition troubled Emily deeply. Ricky had told her quite definitely that Chiara was not in Rome. Hadn't she gone back to her job in London or to wandering around northern European capitals? Had Ricky lied to her? If he had lied, why had he done so? It made no sense whatsoever. Emily glanced back – no sign of Chiara now. Could she be in Rome without Ricky knowing? Did Chiara perhaps want to attack her? Had Chiara in fact called her at the hotel in order to threaten her? Ricky had said they had quarrelled, that his relationship with Chiara was definitely over, letting her imagine for a brief glorious instant that sharing a kiss at the farmhouse had actually meant the beginning of something, not simply the end of a nightmare.

She had arrived at the school. Glancing up at the outside of the building, she noticed a Union Jack fluttering outside the second floor window, where the school was located. She was hanging around on the doorstep, feeling hesitant, when Bill Pickett himself came by, smiling nervously at her. He glanced up and down the street and stepped quickly forward to open the door for her.

"Good to see you, my dear. Well, you'll soon be busy. We might even need to get another new teacher," he said, making conversation as they went up together in the lift – one of the light bulbs was broken and the automatic doors made a loud creaking noise when they opened on the second floor.

Emily thought her new boss was looking rather pale and even thinner than she remembered. He had difficulty finding the right key for the school.

"Would you like some tea?" he said once he had finally managed to open the door. "I have an extra special blend I get from Babington's Tea Rooms. You must go there if you haven't done so already."

He sat down behind his large oval desk and started polishing his glasses; what he really wanted to do was to ask Emily all about the nature of her acquaintance with Ricky Brown. Instead, he said in a brisk tone of voice.

"Come on, let me show you the school!"

He took her down a corridor on the right into what must be the teachers' common room. Bill Pickett was suddenly in his element when he had to explain to her how he had managed to acquire his own school in Rome and how it now worked. He genuinely loved teaching English and was sorry that so much of his time was now taken up with paperwork.

"Teaching is my real passion," he said. "As well as collecting first editions and stamps. And my parrots of course."

"How did you end up in Rome?" asked Emily curiously.

"Oh, that's a long story," he said, staring out of the window, where the Tiber could be glimpsed not far off, glassily still.

"In a way, it was quite by accident. My father used to be a sheep farmer in the Borders, would you believe – spent his life standing in the drizzle, if not getting downright sodden and up to his knees in mud. After he died, my mother sold the farm at once and moved back down to the south of England. I never fancied following in his footsteps. Can you blame me?"

Emily was looking at the shelves that overflowed with books of every description. There were even piles of books, front covers dotted with coffee stains, stacked on a large table in the corner of the room. In another corner, there were enormous, brightly-coloured buckets, filled to the brim this time with children's picture books.

"I never could stand getting dirty or even doing anything very physical. I used to have to go to watch my brother playing rugby for the local team and I would get soaking wet. Put me off British weather for life, I suppose! That must be why I came to Italy in the first place, that and the cooking."

While he was talking on and on (or so it seemed to Emily), he boiled an electric kettle and opened a packet of chocolate digestives. She did rather wonder why he was making such a fuss over her. She was not to know he was trying to win her trust.

"Are you here on your own then?" he finally asked her.

She nodded tentatively, with downcast eyes.

"Completely, I mean. No friends here to speak of?"

"No, not really," she said, such a vague answer only serving to whet his curiosity.

Suddenly, there was a loud guffaw of laughter from the corridor and Monica poked her head around the door.

"Monica Senese," she said, shaking Emily's hand firmly.

The young woman somehow reminded Emily of Grazia, something in the way she looked at both of them with a steely expression that bespoke no nonsense. As a matter of fact, Bill looked suitably daunted.

"Why don't you come and meet my colleague, Sabrina," she said in perfect English. "We can run over the administrative details with you and you must meet Rosemary, our director of studies, as I'm sure Mr. Pickett has already told you."

She looked her employer up and down contemptuously. Emily met Sabrina and filled in various forms that passed from one hand to another, including those of Bill, who was hovering in front of Sabrina's desk. He kept nodding and smiling at a group of middle-aged women who had come in together and were now making a companionable din in the waiting room.

"Do you have connections in Italy then? That must be an Italian surname."

"Well, my grandfather was Italian," said Emily hesitantly. "From a tiny town in Tuscany, I believe, but that was all a long time ago. I'm not Italian, if that's what you mean. I'm a native English speaker." Emily felt she should defend herself. "My mother's surname was Carter – you can put that down if you like."

"No, no, not at all," said Bill, a musing gleam in his eyes. "I've had plenty of English teachers here with Italian surnames. If I'm not mistaken now, "Crespi" was the name of a well-known politician from the period of Italy's unification. Well, maybe it wasn't "Crespi", more like "Crispi"."

Emily had never heard mention of any "famous politician" with her surname and was staring at a print of Van Gogh's 'Arlésienne' on the wall. Bill turned around at the opening of the front door, his good-natured expression suddenly freezing.

"Professor Ignazi, I certainly wasn't expecting to see you here. Shall we go into my office – just the two of us?"

The *professore* glanced searchingly around him, his gaze coming to fall on the chattering ladies who filled the waiting room.

"What a beautiful school you have," he said. "I liked the flag outside too. You should have your national anthem playing – wouldn't that be a nice touch. 'God Save the Queen'– it would be too lovely!"

The *professore* was an admirer of all things British, in memory of his beloved Mr. Fuller of days gone by. He kept on enthusing and Monica glanced in his direction.

"If it's not parrots, it's crazy old men!" she said openly in Emily's hearing. "What a complete idiot!"

Monica shook her head and both secretaries laughed. Sabrina smiled archly at Emily, who felt a bit disconcerted. She had time to study Sabrina's desk, which contained an enormous array of stationery together with an assortment of luridly coloured pincushions in all different shapes and sizes, above all love hearts and miniature animals.

"We should at least give him some credit for amusement value!" said Sabrina, continuing to snigger over Emily's forms. The two secretaries then began to talk about a recent pop concert and Monica's forthcoming wedding in Tivoli.

Emily began to feel a little sorry for Bill Pickett. She had thought he seemed pleasant enough as an employer. Fed up with the secretaries' tittle tattle, she moved away from Sabrina's desk to admire a very beautiful bonsai that took pride of place on the wide windowsill. A middle-aged man, wearing a spotted bowtie, saw his chance and walked over to Sabrina, a haughty expression on his stern features. He started complaining vociferously about the English course he had started and the inadequacy of his young teacher's methodology. Sabrina listened to the man's tirade in silence, her cheeks reddening with annoyance. Finally she rang the bell for the start of lessons and he went away with all the others, as meek as a lamb in an instant.

"I can't stand that man!" she said in a strident tone to Monica, who was now standing next to the photocopier, leafing through a bridal magazine and ogling the wedding dresses on display.

"Monica, I've had enough of your wedding for today!" Sabrina suddenly blurted out.

Monica looked offended.

"To think I was going to ask you to be my bridesmaid – I might as well ask the new teacher over there," she said, giving a nod in Emily's direction.

"Oh, don't be silly, Monica," said Sabrina, smiling demurely. "Of course I'll be your bridesmaid... I just don't need to hear all the details every minute of every day."

Bill Pickett appeared around the screen beside the secretaries' desk just at that moment, the *professore* close behind him, an angelic smile on his unhealthily pallid face.

"So we'll use your car then," he was saying. "I'd been thinking of hiring one, even though my driving licence has expired."

"No, no, all the way to Puglia too – it would cost a fortune!"

Emily looked up curiously at the mention of Puglia, Grazia's plight ever present in her thoughts. She stepped forward.

"Oh, I've just spent the summer in Puglia," she said simply. "In the countryside near Foggia."

The *professore* looked very curious.

"That's where I come from," he said. "Celenza della Valle, to be exact."

Emily could hardly believe her ears as the old man's eyes began to glisten at the very mention of his own birthplace.

"I haven't been back there for more than twenty years. My kind friend here is going to take me back there in his car. I want to see my little sisters again, you see. Poor Lucia isn't well."

"Come along, Professor Ignazi, I'll drive you home now if you like," interrupted Bill, dreading an embarrassing, grief-stricken display of sentiment in front of his new teacher.

"My name's Giovanni Battista. He's the patron saint of my town, you know,"

He shook hands heartily with Emily, bowing in front of her with an appreciative flourish. He even managed to make a flattering comment about the colour of Emily's skirt before he was dragged off outside by an impatient Bill.

In the meantime, Emily's mind was already made up. She would take what could only be considered a golden opportunity to grab a lift back to the farmhouse to find out what had happened to Grazia.

CHAPTER 8

LEAVETAKING

And so it was that a few days later Emily said to Ricky she was going away for a few days. In fact, she told him she was going to translate at a business conference in Umbria. He had come out in an allergic rash for something he had eaten and did not pay much attention to what she had to say, too busy feeling sorry for himself and continuing to watch the TV in Emily's room while he helped himself to yet another of her chocolate biscuits. He seemed able to survive on a diet of biscuits and innumerable cups of Nescafé that he made with an electric kettle he had actually gone out and bought, bitterly bewailing the lack of such an essential appliance in any Italian hotel, whether luxurious or cheap. American soap operas transfixed him to an armchair for the rest of the time. She had only seen him eating anything more substantial once, when the waiter had told him off for helping himself to some *zuppa inglese* from the meagre dinner buffet. The same waiter had immediately reported Ricky's errant behaviour to the hotel manager who had, in his usual condescendingly oily manner, promptly berated Emily. Emily dutifully informed Ricky, in a very roundabout way; he sat perched on the edge of the bed, massaging his itchy elbows and looking at her from half-closed lids.

"You shouldn't really be here, Ricky. I mean, this is a hotel after all and this is really a single room."

"Are you throwing me out then, Emily?" he asked, almost in bafflement. "I thought we were friends. Well, I suppose I thought we were more than just friends. Why have you changed?"

He grabbed Emily's hand and began stroking it, much to her distress, a suitably melancholy expression clouding his beautiful grey eyes. When she promptly took her hand away, he looked askance.

"I thought you were delighted I was here. I thought we could be together."

"I don't know, Ricky. I'm just a bit confused, that's all. Your turning up here was so unexpected."

Ricky's face darkened into a scowl and he took a step forward to grab Emily's wrist.

"What's the matter with you?" he said, bringing his angry face very close to hers.

Emily pulled away, beginning to feel anxious.

"I don't know if I trust you anymore!" she cried. "You seem different somehow…"

"Ah yes, different from our little escapade in the countryside. What an interesting summer we had there, eh? Would you like to go back then? Spend the winter there with me?"

Emily could hardly imagine anything she would have enjoyed less and felt like flinching at his touch.

He pulled away from her at last and began to roll himself another joint. Emily moved over to the window, covering one side of her face with her hand and groping for a way out of the predicament she now found herself in. She wanted him out of her life.

"That's a lot of luggage you're taking for a long weekend, isn't it?"

Ricky pointed at the large holdall she had put down at the door.

"Oh, well, if you knew me better, you'd know I've never been able to travel lightly. It doesn't look like much to me."

"Three days in Umbria then – I could come along. I know this guy in Perugia. From Belfast."

Emily's heart stopped.

"There'd be absolutely no point doing that, Ricky. I'm going to be terribly busy the whole time I'm there."

"Perhaps they could take me on too, as a translator. I mean, I could do with some spare cash. I'll have to get a job, I guess."

"They prefer female interpreters, I've been told!"

"Oh, really, are you sure it's just translating you have to do!" he said, laughing derisively. "Well, if that's the case, I suppose I'll just have to fall back on the old ads for bar staff, although, to be honest, I can't be bothered! Any teaching jobs at that school I told you about? The Shelley School of English – sounds quite posh, doesn't it?"

For a brief instant, he wondered how that old fool of the school director was. What was his name again? Pickett – what kind of a surname was that anyway?

"No teaching jobs then?"

Emily shook her head. He made no attempt to help her with her bag. Slumping down on to the armchair again, he gave her a cursory wave and pointed the remote control at the TV once more.

Emily dragged her bag downstairs and found the manager in the middle of straightening a vase filled with garishly coloured plastic tulips.

"Oh, you're leaving us, are you?" he said, revealing his perfectly white false teeth in a fake smile.

Emily hesitated.

"Not quite yet. I'm going away for a few days."

"Without your friend? You'll be charged extra, you know."

"I thought I might be. Anyway, he's remaining here."

The manager affected surprise, at the same time standing as straight as possible to make himself look a little taller. He was at least a head shorter than Emily who was easily able to look over his immaculate black hair, glistening in the artificial electric light.

"He cannot just do whatever he likes here. I believe you are aware of what he did in the dining room. You quite distinctly informed me you would not have dinner while you were staying at the hotel."

"Oh yes, you already told me all about the *zuppa inglese* episode. My friend said it was the most wonderful dessert he'd ever tasted."

The manager looked thunderstruck.

"Oh, well, I forgot to mention he's a freelance journalist," she said, lying blithely. "He writes a food column in the newspaper too. It's been known to close down restaurants."

Emily managed not to laugh as she spoke and she left the manager looking after her with a delightfully mollified expression on his face.

CHAPTER 9

PUGLIA

The car finally drew up at the bottom of a hillock Emily thought looked vaguely familiar. Giambattista, as he insisted they call him, kept glancing inquiringly in her direction; ever since they had left Rome, he had been trying to worm his way into her confidence. He talked constantly; she had heard all about his boyhood town, his first covert boyfriends, his flight to Rome, the English lover who had adored him, the teaching of philosophy, the headmistress he had wholeheartedly detested, his fall from grace and the difficulty of making ends meet in his ever so lonely old age. Bill, having heard it all before, paid little heed to this retelling of his life story.

The old man was a terribly fussy travelling companion. Bill was not allowed to open any windows, despite it being such a warm day, because Giambattista suffered too much whenever there was the slightest draught. In a querulous voice, he complained about Bill switching on the radio because the slightest crackling disturbance gave him a headache. With a sigh, Bill handed Emily a Shirley Bassey CD to put back inside its cover.

"Please be very careful with that. It's one of her harder to find recordings," he said, sounding overly anxious.

Then his expression of bland courtesy returned and he only looked heavenwards once the entire journey.

"I can't go back," said Giambattista suddenly, wiping away a tear. "People there will laugh behind my back, I know they will!"

"You can't be serious," said Bill, pushing open the car door and getting out to stretch his long legs. "Even if it's hard, it's something you have to do. You're facing up to the past, you're seeing your sister, perhaps for the last time – surely she's worth the effort."

Giambattista nodded his head meekly and hoisted himself out of the car; he had become so stiff from sitting in the same position he practically stumbled as soon as he started walking. There was an abundance of ripe green grapes in this area and Giambattista began eating them off the vine. Bill looked around him, expecting to see an irate peasant bearing down upon them any moment. The old man ate so many Bill felt obliged to tell him to stop so that they could arrive in Celenza before dusk.

"Where is it you wanted to go exactly, Emily?" asked Bill, turning back to look at her; she had been rather silent throughout the long journey.

"It's outside the town itself. In the heart of the countryside, really."

She sounded strangely reticent and Bill's curiosity was aroused.

"But you do remember how to get there, don't you? You'll be able to tell me in good time when to turn off? The roads are pretty terrible."

"Oh, you don't need to take me up to the door. I can easily walk from the town."

"Not at all," said Bill with a wave of his hand. "And, if you'll forgive me, I'm curious to meet this cousin of yours."

"Second or third cousin really."

"Same thing," snapped Giambattista irritably.

The house was empty. No sign of life whatsoever apart from the occasional lizard darting up the white walls or scuttling away from the clay path that was littered with gigantic curled-up leaves from the old fig tree. Emily knocked on the door to no avail, finally walking around the dismal house and peering up at the shuttered windows. The place was eerily silent; even the magpies seemed to have left and the cicadas had given up their interminable drone.

"Looks like nobody's at home," Bill called out from behind the steering wheel.

Giambattista peered out into the sunlight, his eyes watering. He was too busy moaning about autumnal mosquitoes to pay much attention.

"No, I don't understand it at all," said Emily, shrugging her shoulders and walking back to the car. "There's an old man who lives nearby – perhaps he knows where everybody's gone."

"Hop in. Where do I go from here?" asked Bill, thoroughly enjoying his unexpected jaunt into the wilds of southern Italy. In spite of having spent a lifetime in Rome, that most sophisticated of cities, he had, after all, spent his early boyhood in the countryside.

Was it just Emily's imagination or did Pino Giocondo literally change colour when he caught sight of her? He had been cooking and the smell of roasting meat hung about the house, or rather about the low ceiling of the doorway where he stood in his mud-stained trousers, implacable in his silence. No, he did not know anyone called Toni Cellamare nor did he remember when the *casale* had last been lived in. After all, he was only a poor ignorant peasant who kept himself to himself. Emily stared at him, not knowing what to say, totally unable to understand why the man was lying. Pino took one last glance at them and shut the door in her face. She turned around slowly to face Bill.

"He's not telling the truth," she said simply. "I can't understand why."

"Let's go to the town now, shall we?" said Bill. "You can always try again in the morning. He probably just doesn't like being disturbed at this time of day."

In an imposing villa flanked by orange trees and wrought-iron railings, Giambattista's elderly sister lived alone now with two dogs that growled menacingly as they all got out of the car. It was an emotional reunion, Giambattista's sister, quite overcome, clawing tenderly at his face with her wrinkled hands and tears of joy streaming down both sets of furrowed old cheeks, while she exclaimed *Madonna santa* and *mamma mia* several times over. The pair of them prattled on and on, Lucia Ignazi leading the way into her splendid house and insisting that there was plenty of room for everybody.

CHAPTER 10

SUSPECT

Grazia's Milan number rang out. Nobody at home there either. She always had her mobile number switched off in any case. Emily was at a complete loss to understand what it all meant. Why not tell her that they were going to be leaving the farmhouse? Grazia could have phoned her at the hotel after all or had she done so? There had been that one phone call for her now, she remembered, but surely she could have left her a number to call back. Feeling all the while as if she had come here on a fool's errand, Emily found she was being invited to an interminable number of very delicious meals. Lucia, now that she had finally been reunited with her brother, was determined not to let him go. The poor country woman had suffered the anguish of an unhappy marriage for thirty-five long years until she had at last been freed by Matteo leaving her for a younger woman of Eastern European origin, as yet, thanks largely to the language barrier, entirely ignorant of the full extent of his small-mindedness and petty tyrannical nature. Her husband had in fact done his very best to poison her mind against his "depraved" brother-in-law and she still avoided any mention of Giambattista's own love life while she held his age-mottled hand and led him, in elated mood, around the beautiful garden she tended with evident passion, tears very often trickling down her wrinkled cheeks.

Bill, in a reflective turn of mind, sat outside on a wrought-iron bench, sunning himself in a corner of the garden where he had already confided to Emily he felt a poetical inspiration coming upon him. He showed not the slightest inclination of wanting to give her a lift back to the farmhouse and Emily decided to walk there, despite Lucia's protestation that she would not be back in time for lunch and that the way she cooked aubergines was second to none in the whole region. Only her Sicilian grandmother from Catania could have made them better but she had been dead many a long year. Did Giambattista remember *Nonna Maria*? And off they went again on another nostalgia trip. Of course Giambattista remembered *Nonna Ada* too with her imposing Roman nose and her hairpins at the ready to stab his bare thighs whenever he got up to mischief and what about *Zio Gustavo* with the military moustache who had fought in the African campaign. What on earth had become of him?

Without anyone paying her any more attention and with the blare of Lucia's beloved quiz shows still ringing in her ears, Emily set off along the well-signposted road that led towards to the little town where the eucalyptus trees had taken on a golden autumnal hue in the still warm southern sun and occasional lizards scurried away at her approach. It was easy enough for her to find the road, little more than a mud track that led down to Pino's tumbledown house. He was sitting outside in the sunshine, a basket of chestnuts at his feet, smoking a cigarette, almost as if he had been expecting her arrival. A small mongrel barked at her ankles before clambering up on to Pino's lap where they both eyed her with stony distrust, Pino finally gracing her with a grunt of recognition.

"I might have known you'd be back to see me," he said, puffing leisurely on his cigarette, his eyes as cold as ice in his furrowed old face.

"Yes, I wanted to know why you had to lie to me," she said so abruptly her words seemed to crack the air.

"You weren't alone," he said. "Who were those people you were with? I'm not having complete strangers spying on me."

Emily was nonplussed. Was he actually going to tell her what he knew now that Bill and Giambattista were safely out of the way?

"No, no, don't start thinking I know anything whatsoever. No, no... the nuns at Santa Chiara would say exactly the same. Religion will always go washing its hands of some kinds of people and make no mistake about that. Washing its hands of the entire Cellamare race, that's for sure."

His voice trailed off.

"What on earth are you talking about? What's to know? I was here all the summer with my... friends and now the house is completely empty. How could you say it hadn't been lived in for years?"

Pino began to chuckle softly in a very unpleasant way until he finally burst out into a wild fit of laughter that made Emily feel like running away there and then.

"The way Enrico used to live in it too and look what happened to him. That place must have a curse on it!"

"I don't know what you're talking about."

"Of course you don't. But he was the best of a bad bunch, I can tell you! What's it to you anyway? It's nothing to me either now that I can have my vines back on that sunny slope. That land belonged to my family."

"I just want to know what's happened to my friends."

"Friends! A fine bunch of 'friends' you've got, *signorina*. Oh, they all love each other so much!"

He laughed again, making Emily feel more and more flustered.

"Remember you're involved in this too or have you already forgotten about our Albanian friend? I've told you before not to go snooping around. You're out of your depth here, *inglesina*. Go away and choose your friends more wisely."

Saying this, Pino got up, the mangy dog jumping off his lap and bounding up to Emily with a final bark, and closed the door of his ramshackle house firmly behind him.

Emily stared after him in dismay. Was this all he was going to tell her? The eerie silence of the woods closed menacingly around her, broken only by the sound of crows cawing in the treetops.

She took the well-trodden path back to the Cellamare farmhouse. God knows what she thought she was going to find there except a locked door and shuttered windows staring back at her. Where on earth could Grazia be? She imagined Grazia and Toni alone in that house once Ricky and Chiara had broken up and gone their separate ways. They would have been at each other's throats in no time and then? And then there had been Toni's shotgun to contend with. Emily felt numb at the thought.

Nothing at the farmhouse gave her any clues about what might have happened, nothing whatsoever. Blinking in the bright sunlight, she walked slowly around it, feeling ever more bewildered. Those thick walls gave nothing away. The one place she was able to snoop around was the disused hayloft, accessible even without a key. The same wooden steps she remembered, the same assortment of forgotten firewood, rusty old tools and shadowy miscellaneous rubbish. She lifted up a dank tarpaulin cover with a feeling of ice-cold dread, as if she were really going to discover something terrible. A couple of pails and musty firewood tumbled down at her feet together with cobwebs. Emily jumped back. She hated spiders and suddenly could not wait to be outside in the sunshine. The sound of her ringing footsteps on the rickety wooden staircase caused more scurrying noises and she got out into the open, a little out of breath. There her attention was caught by a bundle of silver twine, glittering in the sunlight. Picking it up, she noticed the ground at the bottom of the slope had been freshly dug and the undergrowth cleared away. Had Pino been at work already? Or somebody else?

The solitary old house stood squarely in front of her, the shuttered windows taunting her in the silence of the clearing and getting her to make up her mind. Before she had practically realised what she was doing, she had forced herself in through a back window where a battered old shutter hung loose and useless. Landing on the floor with a clatter, it took Emily a few minutes to get used to the penumbra of the shuttered house. There was no electricity – someone must have turned it off at the mains and she had no idea where that was. A clap of distant thunder made her jump suddenly and she began to imagine Toni at her back, furious with her for snooping around in search of his murderous intentions.

The kitchen was empty, the rickety chairs arranged neatly around the table and the cupboards bare apart from a couple of old bags of crystallised salt and a half-empty bottle of bleach under the kitchen sink. The pots and pans were stacked away tidily in Grazia's methodical fashion. Emily breathed a sigh of relief. What had she been thinking of? No signs of foul play then. Grazia had got fed up and managed to persuade Toni to go back to Rome or perhaps her old flat in Milan. The most logical explanation. Of course that must be it.

Upstairs, the beds had been made, an enormous musty-smelling quilt Emily had never seen before covering Toni and Grazia's bed. Sunshine glinted quite fiercely through the uneven slats of the old shutters, reflecting off the dressing-table mirror, and she caught sight of a familiar-looking object on the shabby rug next to the bed. Picking up Grazia's Louis Vuitton purse from the floor, she hesitated a moment before opening it but a few coins and an old hairdresser's receipt gave her no clues whatsoever.

She was just admiring the massive antique dressing table with its fly-spotted glass, cumbersome relic of a bygone age, when the sound of keys rattling in the lock downstairs and loud voices broke her reverie and found her instinctively diving under the bed like a terror-stricken child. The next thing she realised was that Ricky and Chiara were coming up the creaking staircase, making a tremendous din as they stumbled in the semi-darkness.

Emily, thankfully enveloped in shadow, could hardly breathe. What were they doing here? So much for them having broken up, she thought, as Chiara's shiny black boots and long swirling skirt paused briefly on the threshold of Toni and Grazia's bedroom before pirouetting onwards to the room next door, leaving expensive scent in her wake.

"Not there either," Emily heard her say to Ricky. "What did I tell you, *amore mio*? It can't be here after all! You must have dropped it somewhere else. What does it matter anyway? A bourgeois object like that! I'd burn them all together with the people that use them!"

The giggling turned into prolonged kissing in the bedroom next door and, in no time at all, to Emily's utter horror, the sounds of their lovemaking became louder and louder, at least Chiara's certainly did. Ricky seemed to make do with a low-key wailing. When the creaking noise from the old bed springs and all the grunting finally stopped, there was laughter and conversation. Aghast, Emily thought she could hear her name being mentioned and strained her ears to understand what it was their muted voices were saying about her.

She closed her eyes, willing herself not to sneeze. There was dust under the heavy old bed that Grazia's energetic sweeping had not managed to dislodge. The rain had begun to beat down and she lay there for what seemed an interminably long time, listening to the sound of raindrops drumming on the roof. She was going to get drenched walking back to old Lucia's house. She would just have to wait until the downpour eased off, always if this pair ever decided to go away. What if they decided to stay the night? Horrible thought that Emily realised, with a heartfelt sigh of relief, was unfounded. There they were again in the corridor, Ricky half-staggering, laughing and whispering love in one another's ears, talking about the car they had rented and where they would like to travel to. The Taj Mahal was mentioned. What she said next chilled the blood in Emily's veins.

"You should have got rid of her, like I told you to. You're far too much of a pushover, Ricky!"

"I couldn't have done that, you know," Emily heard him reply. "She's a silly fool but she didn't deserve to die up there. And she will never talk in any case, believe me. She'd be far too scared. Our testimony against hers."

The next moment they were gone, locking the door behind them, followed by the furious revving of what sounded like a sports car.

Emily breathed deeply. Who had he been talking about? About Grazia maybe or about… Emily. Up where? Had he been talking about the day he had taken her up to the top of the cupola? Was that was he was talking about? Why? What did she know that was so incriminating?

Emily had finally found a comfortable position and she lay still for another moment, just listening to the rain and staring at the floorboards, at the little carved feet of the bedside table, at a piece of paper that protruded from the skirting behind the bed. Reaching out her hand, she gently eased it out from its resting place, thoroughly covered in dust, where it had probably lain undisturbed for decades. A faded old photograph. She turned it over carefully and immediately recognised a young Toni Cellamare staring back at her, the same perfectly-groomed hair and the familiar flashy smile. He had his arm draped round a slightly older version of himself except this man, presumably the mysterious brother that no one ever talked about, was not looking at the camera. He was staring at Toni, a serious expression on his face. The parents, at least Emily imagined that's what they were, must have been looking earnestly at the photographer when the picture was taken, almost as if they had been asked to take a deep breath. Toni's father looked like a hard man, one who would not have thought twice about thrashing his sons, maybe even his wife, who was thin, rather sickly-looking and with a hairstyle that would not have been out of place in the 1930s but must have looked very unfashionable in the 1960s; even her clothes looked like they could have been worn during the war whereas Toni's father looked like he had just stepped off a sidewalk in Hollywood on his way to a big night out. This was the man then who had ruined Pino, seducing his mother or maybe worse and ruining his family or so he had claimed. Emily hardly knew what to believe any more as she struggled up from under the bed, managing to graze herself on the sharp edge of the bedside table in the process

The rain had stopped at last and Emily slipped out of that same back window next to the kitchen that, fortunately, neither Ricky nor Chiara had noticed was ajar. She skipped over the muddy puddles that had formed, pulling her cardigan more tightly around her, and set off along the road, enveloped by leaden tiredness, thinking longingly of the bright welcoming warmth of Lucia's kitchen with Bill's inane, good-natured chatter and telling herself over and over just what a complete and utter fool she was.

CHAPTER 11

BAR TALK

"Africa?" repeated Emily, at an utter loss. "But I don't understand."

Matteo beamed at her, delighted in fact to be the bearer of bad news. He had been so curious to gauge her reaction at first hand that he had jumped at the chance of a meeting.

"It must have been the influence of Don Valerio, you know. He was Francesco's mentor in the seminary and he must have realised there was something amiss here in Rome."

Matteo began to twirl a paper napkin around his finger and complacently surveyed the lively sunlit scene, complete with strolling violin player, which met his eyes. It was a beautiful day, a respite from the pouring rain that was generating floods in the north of Italy and causing the Tiber to rise to worrying levels. He sipped slowly, a drop of nectar since the bar in Piazza S. Eustachio supposedly served the best coffee in Rome, possibly in the entire world, he thought to himself, with the exception of his mother's heavenly beverage of course, as well as that of his dearly beloved grandmother in Frosinone.

As far as Matteo was concerned, it was the love story between Emily and his one-time roommate that had been behind Francesco's unexpected flight to a Jesuit mission in Chad of all the remote places.

"Didn't he leave any message for me at all? Did he not even try to get in touch with his sister?"

"Oh, I don't know about his sister. Surely she would have told you if Francesco had contacted her. You must be such great friends."

Matteo stared at her curiously, savouring his own recollection of Chiara Cellamare's histrionic good looks and waiting for Emily's reaction, perhaps at the very least eyes brimming over with tears. There was nothing of the sort. Her hands cupped around her cappuccino, the English woman was not showing any overt sign of distress.

"Don't you get on with her?" he probed further.

Emily shrugged her shoulders.

She had looked prettier that other time they had met or perhaps it was the bright sunlight that did her no favours and managed to render wan her delicate complexion.

Emily had started teaching at Bill's school and had finally moved out of her hotel, to the general relief of everyone concerned. With more than a hint of asperity, the manager had come to speak to her personally, alluding in a querulous tone of voice to the fact that miscellaneous knickknacks, including a crystal ashtray *di inestimabile valore* had gone missing at the same time as the departure from the premises of her "friend", towards whom he could barely conceal his visceral dislike. Ricky had in fact disappeared without any message to be delivered to her or any trace of even a grubbily hand-written note, taking away with him her digital alarm clock and a tube of toothpaste and leaving behind him only the stale smell of a plastic ashtray, overflowing with cigarette ends and half-smoked joints that the careless tattoo-covered chambermaid had not bothered to notice under the armchair. As she had bent down to get the stinking ashtray, she had pulled out another object that had quite dumbfounded her – a gold Dupont lighter that looked strikingly familiar. What on earth was Ricky doing with Toni's lighter of all things?

"Anyway, you were telling me you had found a job here?" continued Matteo in an insistent tone of voice that was beginning to weary Emily.

He had been so expecting a tearful scene from the spurned lover and had even imagined Emily, if not weeping copiously on his manly shoulder, at least letting slip some snippets of salacious gossip. He had to remind himself he had a reserved Englishwoman in front of him, all nerves of steel and matronly matter-of-factness.

"I have indeed. Oh, here's the boss of the school now. What a coincidence!"

Of course it was nothing of the sort. Emily, dreading this encounter, had dropped a heavy hint to Bill that his presence would be welcome at what was, in any case, everyone's favourite bar and here he was in a blue corduroy jacket, holding a bag of roasted chestnuts and sauntering in their direction in the company of Rosemary and the new teacher with whom Emily was now sharing a flat. Miranda was in fact wearing a short summery dress in November and her bare legs, of a startling whiteness, were attracting any number of glances, particularly from a pair of young *carabinieri* flaunting perfectly tailored, scarlet-striped trousers. Matteo started sweating profusely when he was introduced to her and the lovely Rosemary. Bill could hardly take his eyes off his head teacher either and he sat down next to her in elated mood, paying little attention to Emily. She had, however, been in his thoughts from the moment she had started teaching at his school and he had waited with dread for Ricky's reappearance in the school waiting room. Emily had mentioned this Italian cousin of hers who had mysteriously disappeared, had debated with him about why the Apulian farmhouse was now deserted by all and sundry and had wondered what wily old Pino had been hiding from her, all the way back in his car, having left Giambattista to his sister's tender loving care. Ricky's name had barely been mentioned.

Could he safely assume that he was just a passing acquaintance, a ship in the night that had sailed out of Emily's life without so much as a ripple?

"I think I'll have an *espresso corretto*," he said, beaming suddenly at his table companions.

Setting her William Morris tote bag down under her chair, Miranda looked curiously at him.

"Correct, right? Made the right way, you mean? Isn't that how they always make coffee in Italy?"

"No, it means they add *grappa* or *anice* or something alcoholic anyway," explained Emily, feeling much as a parent might feel indulging a curious child, and doing her best not to feel irritated at the sight of Matteo's condescending smile.

"Oh, you mean like Irish coffee then? Oh yes, Bill, I'll have some of that! With cream on top too."

Bill was in his element when he was showing off his Italian bar expertise to newcomers, pretty ones into the bargain. He could just about feel he had put his skeletons in the closet far behind him, skeletons that in fact included Ricky Brown.

Bill had still been married when he had started chatting to Ricky in one of the sleazy nightclubs he had somehow got into the unfortunate habit of frequenting. He and Marina were by then living very separate lives and he had found consolation in eyeing up the beautiful prancing women on display and, what was worse, the attractive young men who hung out in these disreputable places. Ricky was amongst their number that particular evening and had quickly realised he was being eyed up. Sidling up to Bill at the bar, he had got talking to him, standing very close and apparently offering all sorts of promises with those deceptively docile grey eyes and a fixed stare that would haunt Bill forever. Together they had gone to a motel where, to be honest, nothing much of any note had taken place apart from some clumsy, inconclusive fumblings in the dark. This did not prevent an envelope of very embarrassing photos from being delivered to the school a few days after their encounter, by a beautiful young woman with glossy black hair and a very knowing look. Ricky phoned the school and asked to speak to him shortly afterwards. Cajoling, threatening, laughing, he demanded money, lots of money. Otherwise, the photos would be sent to his wife and pinned up outside the school for the horror, or, more likely, the amusement of all his staff and his precious students.

There was an entire family of them now, sauntering across the square and calling out his name.

"Look, look, it's Mr. Bill," they said, waving their arms at him in unison and the pretty teenage daughter blowing him an affectionate kiss.

His heart swelled and, for one fleeting moment, he had the sensation of holding the entire place, the most beautiful city in the world, in the palm of his hand.

Cursing his plight and dutifully paying up Ricky had been the last he had ever heard of the bastard until that day in September he had caught sight of him in the waiting room of his school, the location and name of which he had felt duty bound to change after that terrible episode. Not that someone like that could not have found out everything there was to know about Bill before ruining his reputation forever. What would he have done then? Run back to his old stepfather, tail between his legs? Not likely! Join his brother in some presumably ramshackle building in the Australian outback? At his age!

"Penny for your thoughts, Bill?" said Emily, giving him a gentle nudge and regarding him with the kindness he had realised he could happily expect from her.

He still hesitated, however, and still felt like replying, stiffly, that he had no need of being mothered by anybody. Miranda was chatting to Matteo, much to the delight of the garrulous seminarist; apparently, her mother was from Dublin and was much in the habit of taking bus tours to Lourdes or Fatima or Medjugorje every summer with her daughters.

Miranda was quite adamant about Lourdes being the best possible pilgrimage site.

A bald-headed waiter momentarily interrupted their chatter, edging past them with folding chairs under his arm. The bar was filling up. Their coffees finally arrived, *corretti and otherwise*, and Matteo had to pick up his carefully folded copy of the *Osservatore Romano* to make way for all the cups.

Bill was still wondering whether he could confide in Emily, whose eyes were now feasting upon the lively scene in the square in front of them. The Roman streets were always bustling at this time of day and, when you got tired of people-gazing, you only had to let your eyes wander to the majestic architecture from every conceivable epoch.

"So you're settling down in the new flat?" he finally ventured.

Emily's bright gaze returned to her table companion and she nodded vigorously.

"Oh yes, everything's just fine, Bill, and very handy for the school."

"And, um, have you been seeing your old friends again at all?"

The question hung in the air, unintentionally awkward and probably hopelessly off the mark. Would she even understand who it actually was he was referring to?

Emily understood only too well but was unsure what to say.

"I haven't seen any of them since before we went to Celenza."

Not strictly true, but she had, for some inexplicable reason, instinctively avoided mentioning Ricky and Chiara's sudden reappearance at the farmhouse. How could she have told Bill or anyone for that matter how she had hidden under the old bed, just like a desperate, terrified animal?

"Nobody at all? That young man you came to the school with?"

"Ricky?" Emily was surprised that Bill remembered him at all. She could not recall ever having introduced them. "Oh, he's left Rome."

"For good? Has he gone back to Ireland then?"

Emily stared at him.

"Ireland? I don't think I mentioned his nationality, did I?

Bill began to stammer.

"Oh, yes, I'm sure you did. You were chatting in the car about this and that when we were with Giambattista."

"Was I? I can't remember. Anyway, he's left Rome now. Left the country, I should think."

"Has he?" Bill tried his best not to sound too relieved.

"If you really want to know what I think, he's gone to India with that Italian girlfriend of his."

There, she had finally said it to someone and the sound of relief in her voice was perfectly palpable.

In the pause that followed, Emily glanced at Matteo, still in rapt conversation with Miranda and Rosemary. They were discussing the merits or not, as far as Matteo was concerned, of cooking that was not Italian. Rosemary's parents in fact ran a Michelin-starred restaurant in Leeds. Rosemary's beautiful blue eyes lit up with enthusiasm when she talked rhapsodically about their award-winning chef, whose salmon terrine or mango and lime cheesecake were second to none. Matteo looked unimpressed. As well he might, thought Bill. Who, in their right mind, would enthuse about salmon terrine, of all the infinite number of fine dishes there were in the world, or lime desserts of any kind? He tried to visualise a mango and gave up.

"What in the world can compare to *bucatini all'amatriciana*?" asked Matteo, looking at Bill, presumably for some masculine approval. He would leave such frivolities as tropical cheesecakes to the ladies.

Bill nodded his vigorous appreciation.

"Absolutely, spiced up with chilli peppers, eh? Quite the best dish in the world," he added.

Bill was in fact beginning to feel hungry and glanced hurriedly at his watch. He wanted to buy himself a sandwich before going back to school but did not feel in any way inclined to offer to buy them for everyone, having already paid for everybody's coffees, including Emily's po-faced acquaintance. What was she doing with a priest, for heaven's sake and such a smug, self-satisfied one at that?

"Oh well, perhaps I should be getting back to school. You know we have that course for primary school teachers."

Rosemary looked immediately enthusiastic. She adored children and, consequently, felt she had a special affinity with any profession that dealt specifically with them.

"You'll have to speak to the headmistress again about that course, Bill. They want to increase the teaching hours, apparently."

Bill was delighted to hear that. More lessons meant more money and he, somehow or other, never quite managed to make enough of that. The alimony payments were really getting out of hand. He had spotted his ex-wife quite recently, coming out of the *Teatro Parioli* in a fur coat he certainly had never given her, hanging on the arm of a younger man.

"Bill, could I just remind you about that textbook order we were supposed to put in last week. It's the second or third time I've spoken to Sabrina about it. I sometimes think she doesn't understand my Italian, but she doesn't understand English either."

Bill gave a snort of indignation.

"Y-y-your I-Italian -is perfect, Rosemary," he said, quite overcome by her loveliness and letting his gaze linger longer than was necessary on her perfect features. "Sabrina is at fault

– she'll be too busy filing her nails to copy out the order, I'm sure."

Rosemary raised her hand to push back her golden hair from her forehead, a diamond engagement ring that had cost much more than just a small fortune, glinting in the sunshine. Emily remembered that Monica had told her that she was engaged to a handsome TV presenter who had once been her student.

"Well, would you mind reminding her, Bill? She's bound to listen to her boss."

He nodded his head, while, at the same time, having serious doubts that Sabrina would pay him the slightest attention. He would dearly love to sack her but knew that this was impossible: her father was a big noise in the bank where he had taken out a substantial loan when he had moved to a bigger, more central location and he could not possibly run the risk of making an enemy there. Sabrina had worked for him for far too long and knew far too much. He suspected she even knew about those terrible photographs and Ricky's blackmailing. He often imagined that was what she and Monica were both sniggering about whenever he walked past or was he simply becoming paranoid. Ricky Brown out of the country, possibly in an altogether different continent – now there was glorious food for thought indeed.

CHAPTER 12

OUT OF THE BLUE

Giulia, twenty-year-old student of architecture, was sitting perched on the worn old sofa, glued to the TV set as if her very life depended upon it, utterly heedless of the storm raging outside. She was wearing a striped tank top that showed off the dragonfly tattoo adorning her tanned shoulder and she was clutching a mobile phone to her chest. Beside her, looking a lot more relaxed but still very interested, sat Miranda, who was nodding her approval as she sipped slowly from a bright red mug of very hot Ovaltine. It was elimination night on the Italian version of "Big Brother" and Alessia Marulli, the presenter of the programme, was furiously flirting with Costantino, last week's favourite contestant, who was now, against all the odds, battling it out with the obnoxious loud-voiced Margherita, who should really have been eliminated two or three weeks ago since she had already been nominated twice. How the mighty are fallen, murmured the two flatmates to each other, silently nursing undying love for the handsome if uncouth factory worker from Brescia, who had repopularised the tighter than tight, blacker than black T-shirt.

"Giorgio Armani can't hold a candle to this guy," announced Giulia in Italian. "Pirelli have apparently signed him up for a calendar."

"What, all in the nude amidst rugged scenery?" enquired Miranda. "When's it coming out?"

"Not sure. Where's the phone anyway. We have to save him. Costantino can't possibly leave the House."

In the kitchen, trying her best to ignore the TV show, Emily's patience was wearing thin. Why would they watch such rubbish? Miranda had an Honours degree in philosophy from Oxford University, for heaven's sake; her father was an English Literature professor, who had named his three daughters, Miranda, Katherine and Viola, after Shakespearean heroines. Miranda would probably tell her she was watching the programme to improve her Italian or some such nonsense and not because she was agog to find out the fate of the various sundry housemates in their desperate quest for fame and fortune.

Emily could hear the dreadful Margherita moaning and whingeing and generally playing up to the cameras big time. Giulia appeared in the kitchen, quite incredulous that Emily was not interested in her favourite programme.

"Mobile phone please?" she suddenly demanded in that abrupt way she had of speaking English.

"My mobile?"

"Yes, yes, we must vote now from different numbers. Margherita must get evicted."

Her curiosity aroused in spite of her misgivings, Emily obediently handed her the mobile phone she had recently acquired and followed Giulia into the living room where she got the surprise of her life.

There on the screen was Giorgio Lanzillotti, the same boyish grin she remembered so well, the same tousled hair that had glinted in the sunlight that memorable day by the lakeside. He even seemed to be having the same mesmerising effect on Alessia Marulli, who was giggling like a schoolgirl despite her forty plus years of age. Emily could not believe her eyes.

"I was just saying, Alessia, that sometimes you get to meet people you know could be enormously important in your life and you make the mistake of letting them go.

"Oh, Giorgio, I imagine you're talking about falling in love, is that right? And what's the name of this lucky woman and where did you meet her?"

"Well, I met this beautiful woman while I was still married, you see. She's older than me."

"Giorgio, you naughty boy!"

Alessia dissolved in explosive giggles.

"Oh, Alessia, I think it was the most wonderful day of my entire life and I let her go, just vanish out of my life!"

Emily was all at once agog. Miranda glanced at her and reflected on how she had never seen her flatmate and fellow teacher looking so entranced and, yes, so becoming.

"Oh, Emily, Giorgio's a good-looking guy, all right," she said, patting her shoulder gently. "He might even win, you know. He'll never get eliminated, that's for sure! Everybody likes him."

"I prefer Costantino," announced Giulia with verve. "He should win with all those muscles!"

Giulia had a stack of *Grande Fratello* magazines on her bedside table, next to a course book she had never opened that was considerably longer than the Bible. She had never missed an episode, having started watching the first series with her twin sister when she was but fourteen and had immediately been hooked. She was thinking of writing Costantino a love letter or at least joining his fan club and fell asleep at night, imagining she was all alone with him in the Jacuzzi of the *Casa*.

"Can't you tell us what this lady's name is, Giorgio?" continued Alessia. "She might be listening at this very moment and all could still be well between the two of you."

"Oh, Alessia, it's not as simple as that. She isn't even Italian so she won't be listening in any case."

With a sharp intake of breath, Emily's heart missed a beat and Miranda gazed curiously at her.

"Emmy, don't tell me you know this handsome guy? Maybe he's talking about you!"

Giulia swivelled around to throw Emily a sidelong glance, all of a sudden sizing up her enigmatic flatmate whom she considered practically a relic of a bygone age. In spite of Emily speaking such fluent Italian, it was Miranda she got on with, perhaps actually as a result of the language barrier between them.

Pouting in what she must have considered an irresistibly sensual manner, Alessia Marulli continued to flirt with Giorgio.

"Go on, Giorgio, tell us her first name at least! Announce to the world your love for this woman!"

In the quiet solemnity of the confession room, he leaned over towards the camera, his handsome face suddenly looming large on the TV screen in their living room.

"Ulrike, I love you!"

Utterly crestfallen, Emily blushed scarlet. Ulrike? Who on earth was she? Surely not? Not that Ulrike?

"Ulrike's not an Italian name. Where's she from, Giorgio?"

"From Frankfurt, Alessia."

In the meantime, Miranda had noticed Emily's glistening eyes and, being quick on the uptake and endowed with an affectionately maternal frame of mind, had lain a comforting hand on Emily's shoulder.

"I'm so sorry, Piero," Giorgio continued. "I really didn't want you to find out this way!"

Alessia looked like she had not enjoyed herself so much in a long time. The hush among the TV audience was palpable too.

"Oh, I hope you're going to tell us who Piero is, Giorgio. Is he a friend of yours? Ulrike's boyfriend perhaps?"

Giorgio had covered his face with his hands and when she finally persuaded him to continue with his story, he looked up at her with tears in his eyes. Emily could still not believe what she was hearing.

"He's my uncle. I mean, don't get me wrong, he's not much older than me really. Don't go getting the wrong idea, Alessia."

Alessia's face had clouded over for a moment. There was only so much embarrassing candour, maudlin sentimentality and incestuous smut prime time television could take – would family skeletons in the closet be too much for viewers or (and she smiled triumphantly to herself) would it make this latest series of *Grande Fratello* break all previous ratings records? She decided to hone in on Giorgio, by now putty in her scheming hands. She might even ask him out herself if he was so very fond of older women.

"Giorgio, Giorgio, this is all coming as rather a revelation, isn't it?"

It was no use. Giorgio was quite overcome and had to be comforted by housemates, Marisa, the long-nosed, shrill-voiced beautician from Naples, and Maria Regina, her best friend in the *Casa*, as the luxurious dwelling was called.

With all the aplomb that she was famous for and a last salacious laugh, Alessia now turned her attention back to the evening's nominations. Miranda's hand still lay, in what she imagined was a comforting way, on Emily's bowed shoulder and it was with great relief that Emily was able to shake it off to take the phone that Giulia had just answered. It was Bill, sounding strangely excited.

"Emily, you're not going to believe this!"

He paused for breath.

"There's been a landslide near the town!"

Emily had stood up and taken the phone out into the darkened hallway.

"What are you talking about? Near Rome?"

"No, no, of course not. Giambattista's just off the phone to me. Just outside Celenza."

Emily felt an inexplicable sense of foreboding.

"How can that have happened, Bill?"

"You know how it's been raining so heavily these past few days? Well, it seems a part of the hillside just slipped away down the gully!"

"The gully?" Emily repeated incredulously.

There was a long pause at the other end of the phone.

"There's more," he said finally. "They've found bodies."

Emily gasped and leaned heavily against the jamb of the door.

"Bill, there are bound to be deaths in a situation like that. There's been a landslide, right?"

"No, no, that's the thing. Apparently they were all already dead, had been for long enough. In fact, two of them were in varying degrees of decomposition and the third one was just skeletal remains. Looks like it will be very hard to identify them. Nobody has ever been reported missing in the area."

She could not speak.

"Hello, are you still there, Emily?"

"Uh huh," she managed to grunt, trying to find the courage to ask the question that was torturing her. "Do they have any idea about the sex of these bodies?"

"Remains, you mean, Emily. Oh, they said…. male, yes, all male remains."

Emily's heartbeat throbbed in her ears. Grazia was OK then, somewhere or other, not bothering to get in touch with her, but at least she was not down a lonely gully in the south of Italy, utterly stone-cold dead. So who did that leave then? The Albanian that Pino had pushed over the edge – and there she only felt a vague sense of ill-ease, nothing more. Should she be feeling anything else? And then? And then what about the other two bodies, skeletons, or whatever? She gasped and, suddenly, in a fraction of a second, understood. It had to be Toni. Self-defence? Had Toni gone berserk on them one day and they had killed him or had they planned it? Had they planned it for a very long time? Grazia, Ricky, perhaps even Chiara? Why? She would never know. They would make sure about that. Her flesh began to creep and she could almost imagine Ricky's breath on her neck, his long sinewy arms around her waist. His long white fingers around her neck?

"Emily, I can't hear you at all! It must be the line. Such appalling weather! Are you sure you're all right?"

Emily could hear Giulia in the living room cheering for Costantino and Margherita throwing a tantrum as the results of that week's eviction were announced.

"Oh yeah, Bill, I'm fine. I'll see you tomorrow. Let me know if Giambattista gets in touch with you again."

She said goodbye and put down the phone, her hand still unsteady and her nerves irremediably jarred. Outside, the torrential rain continued to fall, beating relentlessly against the windowpanes in the darkened hallway.

CHAPTER 13

DEPARTURE

At the beginning, Grazia had found it difficult to get to sleep; she always thought she could hear Toni's voice but then she would wake up and discover she had dreamt it all. In a recurrent dream, they had been sitting around the big table in the kitchen, Toni guzzling on an enormous plate of spaghetti, eating it in such a hurry that strands of tomato-stained pasta were hanging out of his mouth. Chiara was across the table from him, wearing a low-cut dress and laughing her head off. Grazia had woken up, drenched in sweat, relieved to be in bed in her old flat in Via Terenzio Mamiani, statesman (1799-1885), with its familiar view of bustling traffic and high-rise flats. She had bought this flat on the outskirts of Milan with the salary from her first job and remembered with a pang how satisfied she had been at the thought that she was going to make it, all on her own in the big city. A long time ago now and a whole lot of things had changed in her life but one overriding characteristic remained constant – the steely determination that had got her away from the provinces and was now going to take her to New York. She had finally accepted the lucrative marketing job her old firm had been dangling in front of her for over a year. Not that money was any longer an object but they were keen to expand to the

American market and wanted her to go with them. The opportunity had arisen at just the right moment and she smiled again, curled up in pink satin sheets in bed like the proverbial cat that got the cream, listening to the rain streaming down the windowpanes and gazing at the Louis Vuitton suitcases that were already packed and waiting. She would not sell the flat just yet. Later perhaps, she would tell her brother to go ahead and put it on the market. Now she was happy enough that it was there to remind her of how far she had come and how she had managed to overcome so many obstacles, how she had managed to overcome her own conscience. Then she had simply reminded herself of what an unscrupulous surgeon Toni Cellamare had been, of how many lives he had managed to damage, including the lives of his own family, as Ricky had hastened to remind her on that bright sunny morning when Toni had suddenly got it into his head that he would go and have it out with old Pino once and for all. Shortly afterwards, Ricky had taken a walk in the woods too, Toni's shotgun swinging languorously from his shoulder, and Chiara had stood stock still at the kitchen window, her eyes as cold and expressionless as her enigmatic heart.

Grazia had been so much in love for a very little while, a fierce inexplicable passion that had burned itself out in the heat of one summer. Women were silly that way. She thought of Emily, so blithely trusting and unremarkable. When would the poor woman ever wake up? Well, perhaps she would send her a postcard, not from New York, of course – no, somewhere much vaguer, from a weekend trip she would take to Florida or the Niagara Falls, New Orleans perhaps – the possibilities were endless. Emily would finally stop looking for her once she realised that her Italian cousin was safe – home and dry in fact. Not that she was going to give her any address in Manhattan; the last thing she needed would be Emily arriving once more on her doorstep. She could not cope with any more false smiles and fake hospitality and she would tell her brother to act in the same way; he was far too busy in any case to be bothering about distant cousins and, as for his wife, Grazia's dreadful sister-in law with her motley collection of spiteful relatives would know exactly how to tell Emily where to take a hike if her brother was too polite to do the job.

Here he was on the intercom screen, looking every inch the slick city lawyer he was, even if he had put on a few kilos since he had married Gabriella and now had to wear glasses, Valentino frames of course. Grazia dressed quickly and opened the door to give her big brother an affectionate hug.

"Oh, don't close the door," he said. "Gabriella's coming. She just went to get some comics for Fernando."

Grazia did her best not to change expression. Fernando too. She had never really forgiven her obnoxious nephew for throwing a baseball glove at one of her precious bookcases, shattering its glass front to smithereens. This was a send-off party she had not been expecting.

The sound of clicking heels on the porphyry staircase and Gabriella appeared on the threshold with a neat package of beribboned pastries, smug and impeccable in a creamy Burberry raincoat and looking fifteen years younger than the age she really was, thanks to a better cosmetic surgeon than Grazia had been able to find. She had certainly come a long way since working behind the perfume counter of *La Rinascente* department store. There she was now, plumping her crocodile-skin Prada handbag down on the nearest chair and coming over to embrace her sister-in-law.

"Oh, we weren't going to let you slip away just like that! Giovanni and I are so thrilled for you, aren't we, *amore*?"

Fernando, eleven years of dreadful exuberance and hopelessly spoilt by both his doting parents, bounded into the room, threw his A.C. Milan scarf at his aunt with barely a nod and jumped on to her white leather sofa without bothering to remove his shoes, almost upsetting the coffee table on its ornate spindly legs.

"*Amore mio*, do try not to get your Ralph Lauren trousers dirty," chided Gabriella, laughing admiringly at her only child's antics and entirely disregarding the potential damage to the designer furniture Grazia had worked so hard to purchase.

"Dear, dear, do you think it will ever stop raining, Grazia? What's the weather like in New York? We'll come to visit, won't we, Giovanni? I have a cousin who has a restaurant just off Times Square."

She suddenly remembered that this cousin, extremely successful by all accounts and American by birth, was descended from the poverty-stricken Sicilian grandfather she tried very hard never to mention and fell oddly silent on the subject.

Fernando had taken a video game from his pocket and was quickly absorbed in it, the incessant sound of guns shooting quickly starting to give Grazia an infernal headache. With a fleeting smile, she got up to make coffee.

"I'm going to leave you a bunch of keys, Giovanni. I mean, I think I will sell this flat eventually. Perhaps I'll make America my permanent home. Who knows? I've always loved New York. Do you remember the first time we went there, Giovanni? *Papà* always complained about the food."

"And the coffee, don't you remember what he said about the coffee?" added Giovanni with a nostalgic chuckle.

Proper *espresso* was now being poured into tiny porcelain cups on a gilt tray and Fernando was taking a connoisseur's interest in the dainty little cakes his mother was now unveiling, laying aside the flourish of Cellophane and crinkly pink and white ribbons deemed necessary to make the products of the *pasticceria* on the corner presentable.

"I don't like almonds. Why do you always get these ones?"

Fernando jutted his chin out and Grazia was afraid he was going to go off on one of his not infrequent tantrums, in spite of the soothing words pronounced by both his parents who gazed at their precious offspring with expressions of maudlin sentimentality. He got up suddenly and headed off towards

Grazia's kitchen from where he reappeared with a large packet of crackers and another of salted peanuts. Grazia watched him popping them into his mouth, one after the other, occasionally missing his target and leaving them scattered where they fell. Then he started on the crackers she had put aside for the plane journey, shoving them into his mouth, one after the other, and amazing his aunt by his voraciousness as he sat, chubbily pasty-faced and for once perfectly still. He would occasionally continue, in a whining voice, to mutter complaints to his mother, his mouth full.

"How's school going?" asked Grazia.

"Don't like it," he replied, hardly glancing in her direction.

"Oh, he's going to another school very soon," interposed Gabriella, taking Fernando's greasy hand in hers.

She leaned over to Grazia and murmured in her ear in an upsurge of sincerity.

"Bullying, I'm afraid. Our poor little lad!"

Grazia tried her best to look sympathetic, doubtful about the truth of this statement. It was more likely on account of Fernando's unimpressive academic record that they had decided to send him to yet another school.

There was a brief pause as Gabriella looked curiously at Grazia, remembering something Giovanni had recently told her.

"We're happy you finally saw the light, aren't we, Giovanni? That terrible man you used to go out with, whatshisname, was not at all suitable for a woman of class like you, Grazia."

Giovanni nodded in happy agreement.

"Oh yes, thank God we've seen the last of him. Not the man for you, I always said that, didn't I, Gabriella? Hard to believe he's a doctor at all!"

"And a southerner to boot," added Gabriella, conveniently forgetting her maternal grandfather from the slums of Palermo. "You can do so much better. I never used to like him and he used to make fun of Fernando's asthma too! What kind of a person would do that? *Ignorante!*"

"Whoever helped you to see the light should win a medal, that's all I can say! They never did find out who tried to shoot him, did they?" asked Giovanni, absent-mindedly giving Fernando's dark mop of hair a gentle tug.

"Oh, the police investigations never really made much headway, I'm afraid," said Grazia with a wave of her hand to dismiss the matter.

"I bet whatshisname was a Communist in any case."

Grazia laughed at her brother's stern expression.

"Hardly, Giovanni. His father was the local party secretary for the Fascists. Quite the little provincial Mussolini, if you must know!"

"Really? I thought he had some kind of farm in Puglia."

"Yes, he did. Didn't mean he thought the farm labourers should have a vote, quite the opposite! I was told, quite categorically by a local man that Vincenzo Cellamare used to wear a uniform just like a soldier and strut around town in military boots. He used to send out his *squadristi* to beat people up. Sometimes people died from the beatings!"

Such unpleasant reminders of Italy's Fascist past had Giovanni turning very pale. He took off his glasses and pinched the bridge of his nose in a gesture that managed to remind Grazia of their teenage years, Giovanni always studying, ever the perfect son as he was now the perfect husband. Fernando was finally listening in rapt attention to the interesting turn the conversation had taken. The constant sound of shoot-outs had ceased and there was a palpable silence in Grazia's living room.

Gabriella, whose family on her father's side kept their own dark secrets from the Second World War, pursed her lips tightly and started to zip up Fernando's anorak for him and rummage around noisily for his woolly bobble hat in her handbag. They got up in silence.

Gabriella's eyes misted over for the occasion and, as she embraced her, she graced her husband's little sister with luminous loving eyes and her most becoming smile.

"We'll all spend New Year in the US, just you see if we don't!"

Fernando went out of the door behind his mother without so much as a backward glance. Giovanni, clearing his throat, turned around to face his sister and put a reassuring hand on her shoulder as she handed him a bunch of spare keys.

"Any problems, Grazia, of any kind, of any nature whatsoever, please just give me a ring, you know that, don't you? I can still give you that lift to the airport if you want."

Grazia shook her head; she had already called a taxi – it would arrive in twenty minutes. Everything had been taken care of and Giovanni was not to worry about anything. When she closed the door behind him, she was still smiling. It was wonderful, the way her big brother had always looked out for her and was willing to continue to do so, but this time his help was really not going to be necessary.

CHAPTER 14

BRIEF ENCOUNTER

What with the landslide causing almost twenty deaths and the immediate evacuation of over a hundred villagers from their dwellings, nobody gave undue importance to the discovery of three bodies cum skeletal remains whose deaths all preceded the present momentous event. Celenza was not even the only place to be affected by the torrential rains. Two much bigger towns, just a stone's throw from the ruins of Pompeii, had narrowly avoided being swept away in a gigantic mudslide that had swallowed up roads and bridges and left utter chaos in its wake. People there had been reported missing in the area and deaths were very likely.

Thus Bill had been unable to get any more news out of Giambattista, particularly when it was discovered that his erstwhile brother-in-law had been named as one of the unfortunate victims. Now he had the full-time job of comforting his sister and had every intention of settling permanently in Celenza or what was left of it. As long as Grazia was not one of those bodies down the gully, what was there for Emily to be distressed about in any case? This was Bill's theory at least, which he was very happy to expound to her on the way to Leonardo da Vinci airport.

"You must surely have heard of that trade union leader from Corleone? The one the Mafia threw down a crevice over a hundred feet deep?"

Emily shook her head.

"Well, when the fire brigade finally discovered his body, well, what was left of it, I mean, they brought up sackfuls and sackfuls of bones. Apparently, it was the Mafia's dumping ground for all and sundry. Not that they ever went to the bother of finding out who was responsible. How could they ever? Far too many dark deeds to ever give a damn, really..."

Bill, in a dark blue crumpled suit and a pair of uncomfortable patent leather shoes, was going back to England for his stepfather's funeral. Big Joe had finally, and certainly not before time, passed away in the old folks' home in Brighton and someone would have to wind up the business. Aaron was certainly not going to be coming back from Australia any time soon and, in any case, Bill's brother had possibly even worse memories of the wily old man than Bill had. He was, however, rather gleeful at the prospect of some badly needed cash. Surely the old bastard must have left something and who could he have left it to, if not his two stepsons. He had no children of his own and had managed to outlive his unmarried sister by many years.

"Brighton you said, Bill? I was once offered a teaching job in a secondary school near Brighton."

"Were you? I had a friend who ran a summer school near the Royal Pavilion. There are so many of them. Peter something, I forget the name. Must be a very old man by now."

Emily glanced quickly at Bill, who always drove his old Ford Escort in an apparently erratic fashion, horn blaring in true Neapolitan style, overtaking and often swerving to avoid the mangled bodies of the few unfortunate stray cats that had erroneously wandered on to the dual carriageway, chock-a-block with speeding lorries and garishly-coloured tourist buses. Emily had kindly offered to drive the car back to Bill's garage rather than leaving it there at the airport at exorbitant expense.

"I am sorry about your father passing away so suddenly, Bill," ventured Emily.

"Stepfather," he corrected, putting a hand through what was left of his bristly grey hair. "Couldn't stand the man."

Emily was at a loss for what to say. She had had a relatively happy cheerful childhood and found it hard to imagine things otherwise for other less fortunate children.

"But you're still going to his funeral, Bill."

He smiled grimly but said nothing.

An awkward silence followed, fortunately interrupted by the sight of the airport looming in front of them and a debate about where it would be cheapest to park the car, Bill having offered to buy her a coffee and a sandwich inside the airport.

Threading their way carefully through the throngs of tourists and oversize luggage that modern travellers feel duty-bound to carry with them, Emily had to walk very fast to keep up with Bill, striding ahead and quite forgetful of her. He was too busy musing over the thrashings he and Aaron had had to endure at the hands of Big Joe.

Tempers were wearing thin at the check-in desk when Bill and disgruntled fellow passengers discovered their plane had been delayed by over an hour.

"Typical incompetence," he muttered loudly.

The immaculately-dressed woman behind the desk threw him a dark look that managed at the same time to be strangely alluring and which effectively silenced him and in fact any other complaints that the other passengers were on the point of making. Emily was envious; how wonderful it would be to possess such a look; it might even be worth investing in the most expensive red lipstick on the market. She turned around, scrutinising the area for a likely shop that had a decent cosmetics counter. Instead, her eyes alighted on the newsagent's window, where it seemed that Giorgio

Lanzillotti's handsome smiling face was staring out from the cover of every gossip magazine on the stands. A national celebrity and heartthrob indeed. His perfect features now graced the wall in Giulia's bedroom, since he had replaced Costantino in her fickle affections and looked like he might even be a serious contender for winning this latest edition of Italian Big Brother. Emily had finally earned the respect of her young flatmate as a result and Giulia even brought university friends home to meet the English woman who knew the famous Giorgio. It was interesting how they gathered around her in the kitchen, as if she really were some kind of guru, nineteen-year-old Giuseppina with the pronounced Neapolitan accent, Gabriella who drove her father's Alfa Romeo and spoke with a lisp, even Giulia's twin sister now paid her homage and admiration while Miranda would look on in bemusement in much the same way that Bill was looking at her now.

"Quite the man of the moment, eh!" he said with a chuckle that was directed mainly at Emily's dumbstruck expression. "Well, well, he must have made quite an impression on you, my dear."

She sighed.

"Oh, he just reminded me of an ex-boyfriend, that's all."

"Oh yes, the kind of ex-boyfriend you never quite get over?"

"Something like that, Bill."

He patted her shoulder in that absent-minded way he had while people jostled around them, battling with their hand luggage. The corner of an executive briefcase suddenly caught his knee and he turned around to glare at the dwarf-sized Japanese businessman responsible, entirely oblivious to Bill's pain as he disappeared in the direction of the bureau de change and car rental service.

Bill's irritation was not assuaged in the slightest when they finally reached the bar and he saw the meagre offerings on display there: a very limited selection of sandwiches filled with greasy cheese and salami that had seen the light of day when the airport had first opened. Bill ordered chocolate muffins for them both and insisted on having a cup of tea, hardly a good idea in Italy and certainly never in an airport. A cup of lukewarm water soon appeared with a teabag in its blue wrapper on the saucer.

"You don't need to hang around here all day, Emily," he said, biting into his muffin. "I'm sure you've got better things to do with yourself!"

Emily shook her head. Did she have anything better to do with herself on a Saturday morning? She shrugged her shoulders.

"*Signorina*, you do realise these muffins are stale?"

The attractive young bartender, who could not have been more than eighteen, barely glanced at Bill.

"*I muffin sono vecchi*," Bill repeated more insistently.

"I can speak English," she said in an indignant, heavily-accented voice.

The other bartender, a middle-aged man in an impeccable red apron and sporting a military moustache, was tinkering away with the impossibly shiny Gaggia espresso machine, entirely oblivious to Bill's existence on the other side of the marble-topped bar counter.

"*Toni, come stai?*" called a voice from its furthest away corner.

Emily's blood momentarily froze, hearing that familiar name and she had to forcefully recollect herself to the present. She glanced in the direction of the voice and could not believe her eyes. The beautiful luxuriant hair was thinning and grey, the face was lined now, but the bright dark eyes still managed to make her heart jump.

"*Bentornato a Roma, caro amico mio!*" continued the bartender, all charm and affability towards an old customer who happened to be called Piero Nisi.

"*Dio mio*! Emily!"

His arms were suddenly opening wide to hug her, much to the amazement of Bill, who had just finished off his muffin amidst a lot of grumbling, as well as the bar staff, looking with deep interest upon this affecting reunion scene. A hundred happy memories came flooding back: their favourite restaurant by the river, Emily's love for cats, Piero's inability to ever learn English properly.

"But I can speak English pretty well now," he said with self-assurance as Emily introduced Bill to him. "I've been working in Germany, you know, and the company was an international one."

He paused and Emily wondered what to say, how not to mention the fact that she knew all about Ulrike and Giorgio Lanzillotti, like all the rest of Italy.

"Have you come back to Italy for good then?" she finally asked, trying to sound as casual and disinterested as possible.

"Oh, Emily, I've had to come back for my mother's funeral."

Piero stifled back a tear and looked at the ground. Emily patted his shoulder as she inwardly rejoiced.

"And how...?"

"Heart attack. My father... oh, you can imagine in what kind of a state my poor father is!"

Emily envisaged the once sprightly little man, so used to obeying his wife's orders all his life. Indeed, would he ever manage to recover?

"Just as well there's my sister on hand. She'll keep everybody on the right track, I'm sure."

Isabella Nisi certainly would. If Emily's memory of this bossy boots was anything to go by, she would definitely keep the whole family in order.

"She has the children to think about now of course. The twins will be two years old soon."

How Emily laughed to think of Isabella, all precision and rigour, beset by maternal cares for two, repeat, two toddlers.

"Oh, here she is at long last!"

Immediately they all turned around to see who he was talking about, Emily alarmed at the prospect of meeting Isabella after all these years. But it was not a young woman who confronted them. Instead, they were presented with a large elderly woman bearing down upon them, her formidable figure encased in funereal black, apart from a blue drape that fell diagonally from one shoulder and gave her the vague impression of having won a beauty contest. She was wielding a plush purple handbag, unusual to say the least, that Bill found he could hardly keep his eyes off.

"You must remember me mentioning my aunt in America, Emily? Zia Tramis?"

Emily could not believe what she was hearing.

"Zia Tramis," she repeated, almost in a trance.

"Yes, you must remember me telling you how she was present at Kennedy's assassination in Dallas?"

"Oh, Piero, that's all old stuff," interrupted the redoubtable old lady, plumping her enormous handbag down on the counter and throwing her hands up in the air. "You could have told her what I got up to in the '70s – now there's a decade to remember! What music... Dusty Springfield, Neil Diamond, Shirley Bassey, I met them all, you know!"

"You met Shirley Bassey?" repeated Bill incredulously.

Zia Tramis noticed him, for the first time, and smiled her most disarming smile, revealing the very best that American dentistry could buy.

"Oh yes, I met her too, of course, when my second husband opened the casino. That was just after we'd moved from Santa Barbara. How I miss the Pacific Ocean, I can tell you, and those surfers!"

"You met her?" continued to repeat Bill, suddenly rapt, much to Piero and Emily's amusement.

"Oh, more than once. I introduced her to my hairdresser, in fact – the best in town," she added with a chuckle, patting her own still enviable head of jet black hair with evident satisfaction.

"And where are you from, Mr...?"

"Pickett – oh, but you must call me Bill."

"Bill it is! What a coincidence, like my third husband from Chicago."

She held out her hand and he grasped her plump, beringed fingers as firmly as he could, making her wrinkled face crease into the most affable of smiles. She reminded him of his mother.

"You must call me Nina then. That's actually short for Giovanna but I've never liked that name!"

Bill and Nina were suddenly the oldest and best of friends, particularly when they found out they were both getting the same flight to London that was now being announced over the tannoy. Nina was going to stay in Kensington with another friend of hers in the recording industry. Did Bill know Kensington at all? Perhaps he could take her to a jazz concert while she was there.

Piero and Emily were smiling timidly at each other all this time, the bar filling up and becoming overcrowded and impossibly noisy. Toni the barman was barking out orders to his English-speaking colleague.

"We should be getting a move on, Bill," said Nina, throwing a mink stole over her shoulders in the most nonchalant manner and tucking her elbow under his.

So they were all soon saying their goodbyes as affectionately as possible and Piero and Emily were left staring after Bill and Zia Tramis as they strode off in the direction of passport control.

"Well, that's quite a relief," said Piero softly, turning to Emily and squeezing her hand. "I couldn't wait to be alone with you again. It's been too many years."

"Really, Piero," she said, quite incredulous.

"Do you remember how you broke my heart, Emily?"

She nodded slowly.

"Oh yes, I remember only too well."

"Well, we have a lot of catching up to do."

Emily briefly wondered how much she would ever be able to tell him of the past few months in Italy, of her very peculiar acquaintances, the terrible things that had happened and her current state of utter limbo. But those dark brown eyes were kind and thoughtful as of yore and that was enough.

"What about dinner then? The same restaurant along the river. Don't you remember? It still exists, you know. For old times' sake, I mean?"

His eyes appealed to hers and Emily found herself slowly nodding – twenty-one again, without a care in the world!

Francesco entered the tiny deserted chapel, relieved to find that the small brick building was still quite cool. He was already waking up every morning feeling haggard after yet another night's battle with mosquitoes as well as the heat. The noisy generator was no longer working properly and the electric light came on erratically, if at all.

He mopped his forehead with a large white handkerchief and sat down at a side pew where he could better contemplate the carved wooden cross that was the only form of embellishment in this simple place of worship that the Darfur refugees had managed to build. In his hand he was holding a letter he had already read several times over, appalled as he had been by the awful coarseness of Chiara's language and the realisation of all the terrible things that had taken place at the old farmhouse. She was unscrupulous and unrepentant as she always had been, relieved, happy, and free at last perhaps?

As for their unrepentant grandfather, it hardly mattered any more who Vincenzo Cellamare had bludgeoned to death or whatever else he had done or not done during the war – after all, the war had done so many bad things to so many people – and lots of people had blood on their hands. Not that that made them any less guilty, mused Francesco in the stillness of the little church. Had his own father been tainted somehow by all that badness he had grown up with? Had he absorbed it, growing up with his brother, like Cain and Abel, waiting for his chance to strike down so that he could continue the cycle of violence? Were they all tainted forever and ever in an endless cycle? Was Chiara, who seemed to have been born without a conscience, elated and gloating over what she considered her victory, a victory in the name of "the people", really happy now that she too had blood on her hands? She had called it "justice", justice for the poor patients who had died as a result of their father's dreadful greed, justice for themselves too, a heavy-handed crude form of justice if ever there was one, of the kind favoured by mysterious hit men on mopeds and hired thugs, very much suitable for the likes of Ricky Brown as a matter of fact. What was it the Bible said about the sins of the fathers being visited upon the children? Grandfather Vincenzo had known all about sin and Toni Cellamare had simply carried on the family tradition. Surely the cycle had ended now? In a refugee camp in a barren landscape of scrub bush and sand that got everywhere, with the poor farmers trying to eke out an existence, somewhat like those poverty-stricken farmers in Celenza of his grandfather's generation, Francesco would not have any time on his hands for reflection. Who on earth would be thinking or caring about the Cellamare family in this land of dried mud and sand storms, where the fields were constantly bone dry, the refugees had witnessed genocide, and all one could do was try to survive against any number of pitfalls, here and now. He was just another priest, another foreign do-gooder, trying hopelessly to expiate all their sins.

The first rose-coloured rays of dawn penetrated the little church, lighting up the stark walls with their gentle glow and flooding its single window with dancing scarlet and orange hues. Francesco bowed his head in resignation before the bleak inevitability of it all and began to pray.